CW00505200

"You'll have

"First we ne

to Pete, then ⌐⌐⌐ wⅼ⌐ppeⅾ ner arm around his waist and snuggled in.

He could do no less than put his arm around her waist and nestle her against him. Selfies rocked. "Now what?"

"Click that little symbol in the bottom right corner so the camera focuses on us."

He managed that, and there they were in the frame, Taryn smiling and looking adorable, him looking…dazed and confused, but happy.

"Bring your head down next to mine so our cheeks are almost touching. That's better."

Certainly was.

"Now put your thumb on the shutter in the middle and smile."

He tapped the button with his thumb.

"I don't think that took. I didn't hear the squeal-click."

"Squeal-click?" He looked at her. "What's that?"

She turned her head, which brought her very, very close. She swallowed and her eyelashes fluttered. "The noise it makes when…it takes a picture." Her gaze dropped to his mouth.

A COWBOY'S HOLIDAY

THE MCGAVIN BROTHERS

Vicki Lewis Thompson

Ocean Dance Press

A COWBOY'S HOLIDAY
© 2018 Vicki Lewis Thompson

ISBN: 978-1-946759-59-7

Ocean Dance Press LLC
PO Box 69901
Oro Valley, AZ 85737

Cover art by Kristin Bryant

Visit the author's website at
VickiLewisThompson.com

*Want more cowboys? Check out these other titles by
Vicki Lewis Thompson*

The McGavin Brothers
A Cowboy's Strength
A Cowboy's Honor
A Cowboy's Return
A Cowboy's Heart
A Cowboy's Courage
A Cowboy's Christmas
A Cowboy's Kiss
A Cowboy's Luck
A Cowboy's Charm
A Cowboy's Challenge
A Cowboy's Baby
A Cowboy's Holiday

Thunder Mountain Brotherhood
Midnight Thunder
Thunderstruck
Rolling Like Thunder
A Cowboy Under the Mistletoe
Cowboy All Night
Cowboy After Dark
Cowboy Untamed
Cowboy Unwrapped
In the Cowboy's Arms
Say Yes to the Cowboy
Do You Take This Cowboy?

Sons of Chance
Wanted!
Ambushed!
Claimed!

Should've Been a Cowboy
Cowboy Up
Cowboys Like Us
Long Road Home
Lead Me Home
Feels Like Home
I Cross My Heart
Wild at Heart
The Heart Won't Lie
Cowboys and Angels
Riding High
Riding Hard
Riding Home
A Last Chance Christmas

1

His back to the door, Pete Sawyer tilted the dolly and eased it over the sill into a recently constructed log cabin on the Crimson Clouds Guest Ranch. The interior was still fragrant with the aroma of freshly cut wood. As the ranch's foreman, he normally wouldn't be setting up furniture, but a week before Christmas, he was the sole employee on the premises.

The ranch wouldn't open to customers until next summer, but the six horses in the barn required his daily attention. Just not right this minute.

"Keep coming." Taryn Maroney, the ranch's new owner, stood inside directing him. "I'm glad it fit through the door."

"Me, too." He looked over his shoulder. "Better move. I'm gonna rotate this sucker so I can come in at a better angle."

"Right." She scooted out of the way. "Oh, man, I love that dresser! I knew it would be a tight fit but I had to take the chance. It's gorgeous."

"It is that." She had good taste. The dresser matched the four-poster he'd brought in earlier along with the nightstand. The unassembled bed leaned against the far wall.

The carved wood of the head and footboards appeared rustic at first glance, but the turquoise color rubbed into the design likely had added that extra zero to the price tag. He'd blinked when he'd checked the invoice before he'd loaded up the boxed furniture in Bozeman last week. Now that he'd had a chance to examine the craftsmanship, he was no longer surprised.

He positioned the dolly near the wall. "Is this about where you want it?"

"Let me double check." She moved back and squinted at the configuration. "Yes, that's good."

After sliding it off the dolly, he wrestled it into place. A cold breeze chilled his sweat-dampened hairline as he nudged the dresser tight against the wall. "Better shut the door."

"Right. I was so busy admiring the dresser I forgot." She walked over and closed it. "Ready to set up the bed?"

"Yes, ma'am." He took off his hat, laid it on the dresser and combed his fingers through his hair. Then he pulled his phone out of his back pocket and set it beside his hat. "Just so you know, I might get a call from my dad."

"Oh?" She took off her jacket and laid it on a rocking chair sitting in a corner.

He did likewise, now that the door was shut. "I got a text a little bit ago. Faith McGavin's gone into labor." And he would soon be an honorary uncle to Faith and Cody's baby. Ever since his dad and Kendra had fallen in love, the

Sawyers and the McGavins had become one big happy family.

"Listen, if you want to head off to the hospital, we can postpone—"

"She's having the baby at home, but I don't have to be there."

"You're sure?"

"Absolutely. My dad does, so he can share the moment with Kendra, and I'll bet the entire McGavin clan is gathering at Wild Creek Ranch today. The Sawyer aunties and uncles don't need to show up and add to the confusion, though. Not yet, anyway."

"I see your point." Taryn smiled. "So Faith's finally having that baby. Now we'll find out whether it'll be a boy or a girl."

"At long last." He liked it when she smiled and her brown eyes lit up. He liked a lot of things about her. She was enthusiastic, hardworking and easy on the eye. Her hair was the prettiest shade of auburn he'd ever seen. "Did you bet on which she'd have?"

"I meant to once I found out the profits would go to needy families this Christmas. Just never got around to it. How about you?"

"I did, during the Fourth of July celebration. That's when most people put money on it."

"That celebration looked so amazing." She shoved her hands in the pockets of her jeans. "I'm glad Kendra put pictures on the town website so I could get some idea of what it was like."

"Maybe next summer you can talk your folks into coming here on the Fourth."

"They'll have to if they want to see me. That should be a big weekend for us. I can't be flying off to San Francisco."

"Speaking of flying, did they make it to London okay?"

"Yes, and they're having a blast."

"Good. And that reminds me. Dad and Kendra asked me to find out if you'd like to come to the ranch for Christmas Eve and Christmas dinner the next day."

Her bright smile flashed again. "That would be lovely. I can save my John Wayne marathon and sugar cookie pig-out for another time."

"That sounds like fun, too."

"Yeah, but I'd rather be with your big ol' family."

"Okay, then." He was glad Kendra had thought of it. Taryn shouldn't end up alone on Christmas because of unexpected circumstances.

Her folks had booked their trip before their daughter and what's-his-face had filed for divorce. Pete had heard her ex's name but had chosen not to remember it. Any guy dumb enough to mess up his chance with Taryn wasn't worthy of notice.

"I'll text Kendra and thank her for inviting me. Maybe there's something I could bring."

"She may say she has it covered, but you can always take her a bottle of that red wine they sell at the Guzzling Grizzly."

"I'll do that. Ready to tackle the bed?"

"Yes, ma'am." He turned toward the unassembled bed, moved the footboard to one side and positioned the rails perpendicular to the headboard.

Taryn brought over her toolbox and opened it. "Did I tell you a couple booked this cabin for their honeymoon the first week in June?"

"No, but that's great." He sorted through the packages of bolts, nuts and washers, comparing them to the list provided by the manufacturer.

"That's one reason I wanted to get this done ASAP. I promised to send a picture once I got the furniture in place. They're excited to be the first guests in this cabin."

"They'll be impressed with the bedroom set. I've never seen one like it."

"I think it's my favorite, but wait'll you see the one I got for the other two-person cabin. It has a completely different feel."

He glanced up from the list. "How so?"

"This one's colorful, which I happen to like, but the other one is more subdued. It's massive, though, and sexy in a bold kind of way. When you see it, you'll know what I mean. It's very masculine, a very rugged Western look, so guys might like it better."

"Well, I'm a guy, and I think this one's nice." He took out what he needed from the bags and shoved everything in his pocket. If he'd known he'd be doing this, he would've brought his tool belt from home. "Do you want to work on the footboard or the headboard?"

"Headboard."

"Alrighty. Here you go." After handing her the plastic bags, he picked up the footboard and carried it down to the end of the rail.

"I'm glad you like this one." Crouching inside the bedframe, she inserted bolts in the pre-drilled holes. "I wondered if it was too over-the-top for a manly man's taste."

"We like colorful stuff, too. It appeals to our softer side." He put the bolts in the footboard. "Ready?"

"Yep."

He lifted his end of the rail in tandem with hers as they attached each end.

She looked over her shoulder. "I've decided to name each cabin so returning guests can ask for a specific one."

"Have you got names, yet?" When the footboard was secure, he moved to the other side.

"I'm working on it. Maybe I'll use names of Western towns. The two bigger cabins will be more family oriented, but for the smaller ones I wanted something intimate and sensual. I'm marketing them as the perfect setting for a honeymoon or a romantic weekend."

"I can see that. A cozy cabin surrounded by tall pines, mountain views, a little kitchen for snacks, even a wood-burning fireplace. What more could you want?"

"Just two people crazy in love with each other."

"Yep." If that was a painful subject, she didn't give any indication.

He hadn't learned the details of her divorce until about four months into his tenure here. Her matter-of-fact description had made it sound as if neither of them had suffered from the breakup.

They'd been married less than a year when they'd discovered they didn't suit. Her ex was currently living in Spain and she'd bought out his share of the ranch they'd purchased together as a getaway. Clean break, no hard feelings.

Maybe she was just that practical. Except there was nothing practical about this fantasy bed they were constructing together. He took a wrench from her toolbox and moved around the perimeter tightening all the nuts. Then they laid in the slats, slid in the box spring and added the luxury pillow-top.

She stood back, arms folded, a gleam of satisfaction in her eyes. "Perfect. I can take it from here if you have stuff to do in the barn."

"Aren't you going to put on the bedding?"

"Yes, but you don't have to—"

"It'll go faster with two people." Idle curiosity. That was the only thing prompting him to offer his help. *Yeah, right. You're enjoying this bed project on a whole other level, hotshot.*

All right, he was attracted to her. But near as he could tell, it was a one-sided crush. Clearly she liked working with him, but she'd never flirted. Not once. She wasn't flirting now, either.

"You want to see how it's going to look when it's finished, don't you?"

"As a matter of fact."

"I get that. I stashed the linens and pillows in the bathtub to move them out of the way. Come on back and I'll load you up. It'll take both of us to carry it all. There are six pillows."

"Six?" He followed her to the bathroom.

"Mounds of pillows make a bed more inviting."

"I suppose they do, but I—hey, you weren't kidding." He stared at the tub/shower arrangement. The glass shower door was the only thing keeping the stacked pillows and bedding from tumbling out.

"Come to think of it, we should divide this into several trips. We'll leave the pillows in here for now." She reached into the enclosure. "If you'll take the comforter and blanket and lay them over the rocker, I'll bring the sheets and mattress cover."

"Will do." He left the bathroom, arms full of fluffy material. The turquoise and brown pattern of the comforter resembled a Native American design that would look spectacular on that bed.

She came out of the bathroom with the mattress cover and sheets. "I splurged on the linens. These sheets have some insane thread count and when I saw the pale turquoise I had to have them. They'll coordinate perfectly with the finish on the bed."

"Yes, they will." He'd never slept on high-thread-count sheets, let alone colored ones. In his world, sheets were a utilitarian white, which went with everything. That was if you even cared whether they matched other stuff, which he normally didn't. But Taryn's enthusiasm was catching.

Positioning himself on the far side of the bed, he helped her put on the fitted mattress cover, followed by the sheets, which were silky as a foal's muzzle. Handling them gave him a little buzz of sensual pleasure. Maybe this high-thread-count concept had something going for it. Sliding between those sheets naked would feel great. Making love on them would be even…*whoa. Easy does it, cowboy.*

She retrieved the cream-colored blanket from the rocker and shook it out.

He caught his edge and pulled it into place. "This is a really soft blanket."

"I love this brand. It's the same kind I have on my bed and it gets softer with each washing. Sometimes I take it into the living room and wrap up in it when I'm vegging in front of the fire."

"Cozy." He always left after feeding the horses their dinner, so he hadn't spent any time thinking about how she passed her evenings. Now he probably would.

She brought over the comforter and he tugged his side into place. "Looking good."

"Sure is." She surveyed the bed. "Time for the pillows." Heading back to the bathroom, she handed him half and took the other half.

After putting on the pillowcases, he left all three at the end of the bed. "I have no idea how you plan to arrange these."

"I'm not sure, either. I just wanted a bunch of them. Let me fiddle a bit." She put her pillows at the end, too. "First I want to turn back the covers so it looks inviting." She folded them down several inches.

He stepped aside, hands in his pockets. He'd made his share of beds as a solo effort. A few times he'd help remake one after spending the night with a woman. But this—decorating a beautiful bed so it would appeal to a honeymooning couple—was a first. And it was turning him on.

At first Taryn arranged the pillows in a neat configuration—three across the headboard, two more in front of those and the last one centered. "That's pretty, but I'm not sure it sets the tone I'm looking for." She glanced at him. "What do you think?"

He wasn't about to say. His thoughts were veering toward X-rated. "I'm no expert at this."

"But imagine you were the bridegroom, and you walked into this cabin. What would you like to see?"

"Some disorder." He spoke before he had a chance to censor himself. "I might have the urge to dive into bed with my bride, but if the pillows are neatly stacked, I'd hesitate."

"Yes! That's exactly the problem. It looks structured, not spontaneous."

"You want uninhibited." His blood heated.

"Yes. This is supposed to be a fantasy." She cleared her throat. "It should generate strong emotion."

Could she be getting a little turned on, too? He'd never seen any evidence that he affected her that way. Could just be the bed and the sexy sheets, which would be enough to give anyone ideas.

She took a breath. "But what's the best way to jumble them up?"

"Just do it." He walked over and tossed one at the headboard. Damn, that high thread count made for a very sexy pillowcase. "Like that."

"So just throw them helter-skelter?"

He shrugged. "Better than too neat."

"You're right." She grabbed a pillow and lobbed it in. "Your turn."

He aimed one that nestled close to hers. "Go for it."

This time she put more force into her throw and it smacked against the headboard. She laughed. "Got a little carried away."

"I'll bet you're dangerous in a pillow fight."

"You know it."

"I'm not so bad, myself."

"Prove it." She picked up her last one and opted for a rainbow toss.

He went for speed, and his collided with hers in midair, making her laugh. The pillows went down together, tumbling against the others in complete disarray against the carved headboard. "I like it."

"Are you saying it makes you want to dive into that bed?"

Was she flirting? He met her gaze. Yes, she was. His heart beat faster. "Yes, ma'am. It certainly does. How about you?"

2

Now what? Taryn met his gaze. She'd gotten herself into this so she jolly well better figure out what she wanted to happen next.

Hindsight was twenty-twenty. If she hadn't accepted his offer to help make the bed, she wouldn't be in this fix. Instead, for the first time since she'd hired him, she'd given in to the temptation to flirt. Bad decision.

He was an excellent foreman, the perfect choice to handle the riding stable part of this guest ranch operation. He was also tall, blond and beautiful. But if she allowed herself to get involved with him and it blew up in her face, she'd be out her right-hand man. She couldn't take that chance.

So even if she was fired up, even if he was looking at her as if he could read her mind, she had to put a stop to it.

But how? What would get her out of this sexually charged moment gracefully? Because if she didn't do something fast, he might decide to kiss her. And once that happened, there would be no going back. Unless he turned out to be a lousy kisser. That would cause a whole different set of issues. But he wouldn't be lousy. Not with his sexy—

"Taryn…" He took a step toward her at the same moment his phone chimed.

Saved.

"That's my dad." Breaking eye contact, he walked to the dresser and sucked in a breath before grabbing his phone. "Hey, did she have the baby?" He paused. "That's awesome."

She turned away and steadied her breathing. Close call. Had a little oopsie, a slight lack of judgment, but so what? She was only human.

As Pete continued to chat with his father, she retrieved her jacket and put it on. This activity was finished except for taking a picture. First she'd have to bring in the lamps she'd bought, though. Light was fading from the sky.

Pete ended the call and gave her a smile. "It's a girl."

"Aw." Good. They could move right onto a new topic. "I'll bet Kendra's pumped about that."

"Dad says she's over the moon. And teary-eyed over little Noel Lorraine."

"A Christmas name for a Christmas baby."

"Everybody's excited over there. And Faith's dad…you've met Jim, right?"

"Jim Underwood? Sure have. Nice guy."

"He is. And he's tickled about having a granddaughter because he has such fond memories of raising Faith."

"You probably want to get going, so you can join the celebration." She buttoned her jacket. "I'll feed the horses tonight."

"I'm in no rush. In fact, Dad's told the Sawyer contingent to come over to Wild Creek Ranch about six. He asked me to invite you."

"Me?"

"We need all the folks we can get. The plan is to round up all the McGavins, all the Sawyers, and any other friends we can rope in. Then we'll stand outside Faith and Cody's A-frame and serenade them with Christmas carols for a little while."

"That's so sweet."

"Theoretically, although no telling how it will go down since the Whine and Cheese Club is behind it. I'll bet we'll end up singing stuff like *Grandma Got Run Over by a Reindeer*."

Taryn grinned. "I wouldn't be surprised. They're like slightly twisted fairy godmothers."

"Yeah." He laughed. "Anyway, if you're up for it, there's food involved. You can ride over with me and I'll bring you back here when it's over. Shouldn't go very late."

Ten minutes ago, she wouldn't have hesitated to accept his offer. But she did, now.

He picked up on it. "Unless you'd rather drive yourself."

And what kind of fainting female would that make her? Because of one hot look she couldn't muster the courage to ride in his truck? To hell with that!

She took a calming breath. "I'd love to ride over with you."

"Great."

Maybe it was just that easy. "Where did the Lorraine part come from?"

"That was Faith's mom's name." He glanced at her jacket. "You look ready to leave the cabin. Didn't you want to take pictures?"

"I have to get the lamps, first. They're still in that back bedroom where I've stored everything."

He picked up his jacket and hat. "Then let's go fetch 'em. Might as well take the dolly back, too, so it's ready for the next bedroom set. We could do that one tomorrow afternoon if you want."

"Okay." And she'd just ignore the fizzy sensation in her veins while they did it.

On the way back to the house, she matched her pace to his ground-eating one and their rapid breathing fogged the air. After turning up her collar against a cold wind, she tucked her gloveless hands into her pockets.

The dolly rattled along on the dirt path, making so much noise she had to practically shout to be heard. "Just thought of something else I need to buy—a utility vehicle to haul people and suitcases to the cabins. Could you please check into what's available in the area?"

"Be glad to. My dad and I used UTVs for our horse-breeding operation. They make good little snow plows, too."

"Which I'll need, anyway, especially if I intend to open for two weeks at Christmas next year. I'm still undecided about that."

"Like I said, I'm game if you want to do it."

"But it means we'd both be working during the holiday. Wouldn't you rather be with your family?"

"I could still carve out some time to be with them." He picked up the dolly, carried it to the porch and set it against the railing. "But you couldn't leave to go see yours."

"I could ask them to spend the holidays with me, instead." She opened the massive front door, one of the many things she loved about the house.

"I'll bet they'd like that."

"I think they would. But if I'm going to offer a Christmas package for next year, I need to put it on the website ASAP while people are still in holiday mode. Once I do that, I'm committed to at least that one year."

"But if it turns out you don't like it, you can drop the concept the next year."

"That's what I'm thinking. Do it on a trial basis." She liked to bounce ideas off him. He thought like a businessman because he'd run a breeding stable with his dad before they'd both moved to Eagles Nest.

As she walked through the living room turning on lamps, she breathed in the faint scent of wood smoke from last night's fire. She enjoyed her evenings curled up with a book, a glass of wine and some finger food that passed as dinner. The cook she'd lined up would start working in the spring, and until then, she made do with simple meals.

Pete followed her down the hallway. "I've never been clear on how much of the house the guests will be allowed to use."

She glanced over her shoulder. "That's because I keep changing my mind. My current plan is to allow them access to the living and dining room during the day but close up after dinner, so I'll have some time to myself."

"That sounds reasonable."

"I think so. I put fireplaces in every cabin, so they can still enjoy the coziness of a fire without spending every evening here. But I might designate one night, maybe Saturday, when everyone's welcome to gather in the living room."

"I'll bet that would go over great."

"I think it will. Even in the large hotel I managed in San Francisco, guests loved having a gathering place with access to board games and books. It builds a sense of community."

When they reached the bedroom she was using for furniture storage, she handed him the floor lamp and one of the table lamps. She carried the third lamp and her digital camera. Her phone took relatively decent pictures, but this one was better, especially for images that she wanted to use on her website.

She needed to hire a professional photographer, but she hadn't done it yet. Kendra was a good source of recommendations, but she'd been super busy getting ready for the birth of her first grandchild. Not a good time to ask.

Pete glanced over as they retraced their steps to the cabin. "So are these shades what they call Tiffany?"

"They're in the Tiffany style but they're designed to blend with a Western decorating scheme."

"I like them."

"So do I. That's why I bought quite a few. Now I'm impatient to have some guests so they can enjoy everything I've created."

"That's going to be fun, seeing the reactions."

"I can't wait. I've put my heart into this because I believe people will love it as much as I do. I just need to convey my excitement in the marketing and I'll end up with more business than I know what to do with. Eventually I'll have to build more cabins!"

"I look forward to that day."

For a moment, she allowed herself to savor the warmth in his voice and the gleam in his eyes. "So do I." But when the gleam started to turn into something else, she looked away. If she gave him the slightest encouragement, it would be the dumbest move she could possibly make.

3

Pete believed every word Taryn had said. She had the talent to make Crimson Clouds Ranch into a goldmine. The name she'd hung on it tickled him, though. It sounded more like a day spa than a Montana ranch, but greenhorns might go for a place named Crimson Clouds.

If they booked a cabin, they'd sure as hell gobble up the atmosphere she was creating. She'd confided that she and her ex had made a tidy profit on some real estate in the Bay area during their marriage. She'd used her half of the money for this venture. Her dream for a life with whoozit hadn't panned out, so this was her new dream.

Which was why he needed to be cautious. During that emotional moment in the cabin, she'd looked like she was considering taking their working relationship into personal territory. He'd been onboard with that idea at the time.

Evidently she'd changed her mind. Totally her call. She was his employer, after all. Getting friendly would complicate things. He'd be wise to keep a lid on his libido. Might not be the easiest task in the world, but he'd do it.

That meant enduring a seductive photo shoot in that cozy cabin. While she took pictures, he was her assistant—dimming the lights, pulling back the covers and rumpling the sheets. He could have weaseled out of it by using feeding time as an excuse to leave. He wasn't a weasel.

But staying was torture. He kept moving so the fly of his jeans wouldn't start to pinch.

Luckily she ended the photography session before he embarrassed himself. Stepping into the cold evening air took care of any lingering issue and he was fine by the time they brought the horses in from the pasture.

Taryn had known nothing about horses when she'd taken up residence at this ranch, but she'd been eager to learn. Teaching her had been a joy and a pleasure. They'd bought these horses together, one at a time, and she'd had input on every purchase.

The horse-search outings had been some of his most memorable times with her. She'd been drawn to the beautiful ones, naturally, so that was one reason they had a dappled gray named Fifty Shades and a palomino named Honey Butter. The other four were serviceable chestnuts and much cheaper because they weren't flashy like the other two. At first she'd claimed the chestnuts were like quadruplets and she couldn't tell them apart.

Now she could, though, and her affection for all the horses warmed his heart. She used feeding time to love on each of them. After a few weeks of delivering hay flakes and mucking out stalls under his supervision, she'd managed by herself on his day off.

But she'd have to hire another stable hand once the guests arrived. She'd be too busy to spend much time in the barn. He'd miss having her there sweet-talking those animals. He'd miss being able to spontaneously suggest going for a ride. She was coming along on that skill, too. Another six months and she'd be totally relaxed in the saddle.

"That takes care of that." She pulled off her work gloves as she walked toward him. The barn still had half-a-dozen empty stalls. Room to grow. "Do I have time to freshen up before we leave?"

He took out his phone. "Is ten minutes enough?"

That seemed to amuse her. "You tell me. I haven't looked in a mirror recently. It could be a thirty-minute job for all I know."

He glanced her way. Flushed cheeks, windblown hair, sparkling brown eyes. "Perfect as is."

"Now I know for sure you're full of it. Come on up to the house while I pull a brush through my hair."

"Alrighty." He doused the overheads before they left the barn and then he closed the double doors.

As they started off, Taryn glanced up at the stars glittering above them. "Little Noel Lorraine was considerate, coming into the world when the weather is halfway decent. This plan wouldn't work very well in a blizzard."

"I suppose they could have postponed it."

"But having it on her birthday is the best way to go. I wonder if Kendra and Quinn realize they're setting a precedent. Odds are there will be more grandchildren."

"That's a given."

"But they can't count on having only Christmas babies, so they'll have to figure out a playlist for the ones born the rest of the year."

"And should they be the same tunes, or different ones for the season?"

"Good question." She climbed the porch steps. "My guess is that whoever proposed this concept didn't think too far ahead."

"Caught up in the moment." He followed her into the house.

"It happens. Make yourself at home. I'll be back in a flash."

"Take your time." Knowing her, she wouldn't be gone more than five minutes. He unbuttoned his jacket and glanced around the large living room. He and a high school kid she'd hired for the summer had lugged in most of the furniture. Although it was all new, Taryn had bought classic pieces that looked as if they could have been here for years.

Gradually, with the addition of pillows, lamps and throws, she'd made the space look lived-in. She'd grouped the furniture to form several conversation areas, which would work well if she invited her guests to spend a Saturday night here.

A square table with four armchairs would be perfect for cards or a board game. In another corner, four wingbacks surrounded an oval coffee table for anyone who wanted to just sit and talk.

Two overstuffed chairs flanked a roomy sofa positioned in front of the fireplace.

During their bed-making episode, she'd mentioned wrapping up in her blanket to enjoy the fire. She must have done that last night, because pillows were stacked at the end of the sofa as if she'd used them to lean against while she read the book lying on the side table. Moving closer, he studied the cover. A woman wearing an old-fashioned long dress was in the arms of a cowboy.

"It's a love story set in the Old West."

He glanced up. "Is it any good?"

She walked toward him, lipstick on and hair tamed. "It's exactly what I wanted. I get to escape into a world where I know everything will turn out well in the end."

"I like a good ending, myself." He helped her on with her jacket and opened the door.

She stopped on the porch and took knit gloves from her pocket. "Do you read?"

"Not much, but when I do, I want lots of action and the good guys have to win in the end." He looked at her multicolored gloves. "I don't think I've seen those before."

"My mother made them. And a hat to match." She pulled that out and tugged it over her glossy hair. "I only wear these when I know they won't get messed up."

"They're pretty."

"I think so, too, but mostly I love the idea that she made them for me." She started down the steps.

Something about that hat got to him. It made her look younger and more vulnerable. The store she set by those hand-knit items affected him, too. He walked beside her over to his truck. "She's a knitter, then?"

"She's just getting into it. As you've probably concluded, my family has money. They inherited and then invested wisely. She can buy me all kinds of stuff, and has, but recently she decided it would mean more if she made me a gift."

"Without ever meeting your mom, I like her already."

"My parents are good people. They're devoted to each other, too. Forty-one years together and they're more in love than ever."

"That's special." He opened the passenger door and gripped her hand to help her in. He'd been in the habit of doing that all along whenever they'd taken his truck somewhere. It was the way he'd been taught.

It was one of the few times he'd touched her, though. Riding lessons were the other instance. Until now, he hadn't allowed himself to put any importance on doing it. Those days were over. He treasured the brief contact of her gloved hand in his. Wanted more than that. Couldn't have it.

Once he was behind the wheel, he got the heater going. "It'll be cold standing out in front of that A-frame, but having a crowd of people should help."

"It'll be fun, too. I had such a good time getting to know everybody at Roxanne's wedding last month. Now I get to see them all again tonight and then I can look forward to my first Christmas here."

"It'll be my first one, too. I thought it would be weird not being at the Lazy S for the holidays." He backed out and started down the dirt road. "Instead it's shaping up to be a great Christmas, starting with tonight's deal."

"Will that little cutie Josh be there, do you think?"

"I imagine so." Pete smiled at the thought of his brother Gage's fifteen-month-old son. In September, Josh's mom Emma had arrived in town with a baby Gage hadn't known existed.

"Have Emma and Josh moved here yet?"

"Not yet. Poor Gage is so eager for them to do that, but Emma's easing into it, like the responsible mom she is. Each time she and Josh visit, they stay at Gage's house a little longer than before. They came down this past weekend and plan to stick around through New Year's."

"I wonder what Josh will think of his new baby cousin." She glanced over at him. "Or will these babies be cousins since your dad and Kendra aren't married?"

"Nobody seems to care that they're not married. They're a committed couple, which unites their extended families in spirit, and that's good enough for all of us. So, yes, those two little ones are cousins as far as everyone's concerned."

"That's really nice."

"It tends to be how things work around here." He turned onto the paved two-lane that would take them through town and out to Wild

Creek Ranch. "Faith hopes Emma will move to town so the two babies can spend time together."

"As an only child myself, I understand that. I would have loved to have a brother or sister close to my age, or a cousin. I wouldn't have been picky. I just wanted somebody to play with during family get-togethers."

"You didn't have cousins, either?"

"I did, but my parents had me late in life and my cousins were all a minimum of fifteen years older than me."

"I don't have cousins at all, but at least I had my brothers and my sister."

"Why no cousins?"

"My mom was an only child. And my dad's brother never had kids." He reached the outskirts of town and slowed as he cruised down Main Street, which was dressed up like Christmas Town, USA. The old-fashioned lampposts were decorated with holly and red bows, the storefronts all had wreaths and garlands, and larger garlands hung at intervals across the street.

"Eagles Nest is so pretty decorated like this, especially at night."

"Yeah, the town council does a terrific job."

She turned toward him. "You mentioned your dad has a brother?"

"Yes, ma'am. Uncle Brendan."

"Have I met him? I confess I might have forgotten if I did."

"You haven't met him. He didn't make it to the wedding, and my dad said he was bummed about that, but it couldn't be helped."

"What does he do?"

"He's a wrangler on a guest ranch in Australia. Or jackaroo, I should say."

"No wonder I haven't met him."

"He'd arranged time off to attend the wedding, but a couple of people came down sick and they needed him. They gave him Christmas off, instead."

"He sounds like an interesting guy. Why Australia?"

"Dad says he saw *The Man from Snowy River* as a teenager and was hooked on Australia from then on."

"Great movie. One of my mom's favorites. And mine. It didn't inspire me to head for Australia, but it might have influenced buying the ranch."

"I'm sure glad you ended up here instead of Australia."

"Me, too. I fall more in love with this area every day."

"So do I." And she was one of the reasons.

4

This outing with Pete was the closest Taryn had come to a date in almost two years. And she was liking it a lot. She had no business liking it because she wasn't going to get involved with him, but she couldn't shake the date vibe they had going on.

For the first time since they'd been working together, they were going to a social event. Prior to this they'd either been on a mission to buy a horse or they'd been out picking up supplies for the ranch.

Sometimes they'd grabbed a quick bite to eat while they'd been away from the ranch, but the dynamic had always been work-focused. Tonight, though, was just for fun.

"That's Michael and Roxanne up ahead." Pete flashed his lights and got a quick horn toot in response. "I wonder who the heck's minding the Guzzling Grizzly tonight."

"Maybe they left Tansy in charge." The fuchsia-haired bartender had been on duty several times when she and Pete had gone to the GG for lunch. "I'll bet she could handle things for a couple of hours."

"Yeah, she could and they probably did that. Word's spread about the baby, so nobody will expect the GG to be fully staffed, or Bryce and Nicole to perform like they normally would tonight. Gage is their backup bartender, which is no help in this situation, either."

"Sounds like they might need to hire more people who aren't family."

"Right." As the road curved, Pete glanced in his side-view mirror. "Wes and Ingrid are behind us. Thought that was them. Holy cow. The cars just keep coming around that bend. It's like a rock concert."

She swiveled in her seat. "That's quite a lineup. Think of the stories everyone will tell this little girl when she's older. She'll feel like a princess hearing about this crowd arriving to welcome her into the world."

"I'll bet she'll feel like a princess long before she's old enough to understand what happened tonight. It'll be very good to be Noel Lorraine."

"I hope someone's planning to get a video of this."

"With my dad, Faith's dad and Kendra involved, there will be video. They might even have hired someone."

"If they have, I want to locate him or her and get a card. I'm at the point where I need some professional quality shots of Crimson Clouds."

"I'll be on the lookout, too." He put on his signal and swung the truck onto the Wild Creek Ranch road.

"I may not book it until after the first of the year, but I—oh, wow. Look at all the little white lights they've put up everywhere. The porch, the bushes, the trees, even the barns! It's like a fairyland."

"Sure is. Beautiful. I heard something about lights going up but I haven't been out here at night recently." He slowed. "Will you look at that? Ryker's directing traffic with one of those batons for parking planes at the airport."

"That's funny. Who but a pilot would think of such a thing?"

"Or have access to one? Works, though. Evidently the family anticipated the need for a parking attendant." He rolled down his window. "Hey, Ryker. Where do you want me to put my truck?"

He pointed the baton toward the corral. "Head on down that way. Badger will find you a spot."

"Sounds good."

Taryn leaned across Pete. "The place looks fabulous, Ryker!"

"Thank you, ma'am. Gave us something to do while we waited for Miss Noel Lorraine to show up."

"See you out by the A-frame, bro."

"You bet." Ryker patted the top of the cab. "It'll be great."

As Pete rolled up his window and drove toward the corral, Taryn let out a happy sigh. "It's already great. I love that so many people came out. I'm just beginning to realize how close-knit this community is."

"I didn't get it until Fourth of July. That was my first inkling that Eagles Nest was more than a cute little town. Folks here care about each other. A lot."

"Yes, they do." She counted the cars and trucks up by the house, over in front of the barn and next to the corral, where they were headed. "There's more than fifty vehicles already and they're still coming. You said there was food involved, but I can't imagine how Kendra could feed—"

"Oh, she won't. You're probably looking at the biggest potluck you've ever seen. If I know my dad, he's got the fire pit ready to go with the touch of a match, so we can all converge over at the picnic area by the house."

"Okay, good. I was trying to imagine how she'd handle this crowd in her house."

"She won't try. Her secret to pulling this off is the Whine and Cheese Club. Those ladies will organize the food that folks brought and set up the serving line. It'll go like clockwork. They—excuse me. I need to check with Badger." He rolled down the window again. "Where do I go?"

"Right next to Michael and Roxanne. I'll get in front and wave y'all in like you were a 747 cozyin' up to the jet way."

Pete chuckled. "I think I can manage on my—"

"Not doubtin' you, Pete, but I have my orders. Miss Kendra wants to keep folks from bangin' into her fence. But first let me give y'all your kazoos."

"Kazoos?" Pete started laughing. "Oh, dear God, my dad's behind this, isn't he?"

"Matter of fact, he is." Badger handed over two of the small plastic instruments. "How'd you know?"

"Long story. When are we supposed to play them?"

"I'm not privy to that intel. But you'd best let me wave y'all in. Traffic's stackin' up."

"You got it." Pete handed her the kazoos, one red and one green. "Pick your color."

"Red."

"Good, because I really wanted the green one."

She was still smiling about that when he helped her out of the truck. "Did you have a kazoo when you were a kid?"

"Yes, ma'am."

"Was it green?"

"No, it was yellow. Gage got the green one and I never could talk him out of it."

"Hey, you two." Roxanne came around the back of the truck with Michael right behind her. Pete's sister was tall like all the Sawyers, but she didn't look much like Pete. Instead she had the same dark curly hair and brown eyes as Wes and Gage.

She came forward, hands outstretched. "Taryn, how cool that you're here!" She pulled her in for a quick hug.

"I think so, too. I haven't seen you guys since you got back from your honeymoon. How was Hawaii?"

"Terrific." Roxanne turned and gave her husband a fond glance. "But it's good to be home. Whoops, we'd better move so Wes can park."

Soon afterward Wes and Ingrid piled out of their truck and joined them. Wes glanced at Roxanne. "Gage is coming, right?"

"Last I heard," she said. "Ah, there he is. I don't recognize his truck since he bought that four-door so he could put Josh's car seat in it." She held up her kazoo. "Can any of you play this thing?"

"Of course." Pete took his out of his jacket pocket. "You don't remember Dad getting these for us when we were kids?"

"No."

"Well, he was enamored of them."

"That he was." Wes grinned at him. "And I see you managed to snag a green one this go-round."

"And what did you get?"

Wes held up his blue kazoo. "Got my favorite color. Déjà vu all over again."

Roxanne peered at them. "How are you two remembering all this? I sure don't."

"I don't think you were into it like we were," Pete said.

"Clearly I wasn't."

"Well, this is my first kazoo experience," Taryn said.

"Mine, too." Ingrid held up her red one. "Matches my hat." She waved her hand as Gage and Emma got out of Gage's new truck. "Hey, guys, we're over here!"

"We see you," Gage called out. "Just have to get the little guy out of his car seat."

"Sounds like he needs help." Pete glanced at Taryn. "Excuse me a minute. Gotta go fetch my nephew."

"Hey, big brother," Wes called after him. "If you think you've got first dibs on Josh just because you're heading over there to help, you've got another think—"

Pete turned around and walked backwards as he grinned at Wes. "I don't think. I know."

Roxanne sighed. "Just like old times. He was always one step ahead of us."

"Except that he never got Gage's green kazoo," Wes said.

"Yes, but he's in the catbird seat now," Roxanne said. "He's got first possession of our nephew."

Taryn glanced over at Gage's truck and sure enough, Pete came back carrying that little blondie with Gage and Emma on either side.

Wisps of the baby's flaxen hair stuck out from under the hood of his snowsuit. As Pete made faces at him, Josh giggled and tried to grab Pete's nose, but his mittens foiled his attempts. He ended up patting his uncle's face.

"Good to see you here, Taryn!" Gage called out.

"Hi, Taryn!" Emma pulled up the zipper on her parka. "How are things coming along at your ranch?"

"Pete and I are making good progress. Josh sure looks happy and healthy."

"Yep." Emma smiled. "Growing like a weed."

"Speaking of growing," Gage said, "this crowd is getting huge. We need to hustle or we'll be stuck in the back."

"Alrighty, then." Wes gestured them forward. "Wagons, ho!"

Taryn fell into step beside Pete as they started up a pathway lit by twinkling white lights. "Got yourself a buddy, I see."

"Yes, ma'am. This little guy loves his Uncle Pete. Isn't that right, sport?"

"Pee-pee!"

Taryn choked on a laugh. "Sorry. It's just—"

"I know. But at least he's taking a shot at my name."

"And it's not like that will stick or anything." Gage came up behind them and clapped him on the shoulder. "Right, Uncle Pee-pee?"

Taryn lost it.

5

Pete would tolerate being called Uncle Pee-pee all night long if it made Taryn laugh like that, totally unrestrained with happy tears streaming down her cheeks. She'd never laughed that way before when he'd been around. It was wonderful to see.

She had to stop walking as she struggled for breath, so he stopped, too, along with Gage and Emma. Evidently Taryn was caught in a laughter loop, because every time she looked at him holding Josh, she started giggling again. At this rate neither of them would make it up the incline to where the crowd was gathering.

Better remove the source of hilarity. He turned to Gage. "Guess I need to give him up for a bit."

"Sure thing."

"Thanks. See you, buddy." He gave Josh a quick kiss on the cheek and passed him back to Gage. Then he edged closer to Taryn. "You look a little wobbly."

She gazed up at him, dark eyes sparkling. "Because I am. Haven't laughed like that since...I can't remember."

"It's good for the soul, you know."

"I'm sure it is. I'm just out of breath."

"This might sound quaint and old-fashioned, but how about if you take my arm so I can assist you up the hill?"

"I'd love that." She hooked her arm through his. "Let's go."

He set out, watching for patches of ice left from the last week's snowstorm. Lights strung in the trees on either side of the incline helped with visibility, but the footing was a little tricky. Or so he told himself because he wanted an excuse to keep her close.

"Come on over," Wes called from his place in the crowd. "We made room for you."

"Thanks, bro." His siblings had staked out their turf and left an open space in the middle. He guided Taryn into it. Then he glanced up at the A-frame. Colored lights decorated the roofline and the second-story balcony.

"This is so festive!" Taryn slipped her arm free with a murmur of thanks. "I'm glad you saved us a spot, guys. I had a fit of giggles back there."

Gage gave her an innocent look. "Can't imagine why."

"Some of us got luckier than others with the name thing." Roxanne had appropriated Josh and she leaned down to rub her nose against his. "I get to be Rah-rah. I can live with being called Auntie Rah-rah."

"I'll be sure and reinforce that one, then," Gage said. "Hey, does anybody know the plan?"

"The Whine and Cheese ladies are working their way through the crowd," Emma said. "I assume they're giving everybody instructions."

Pete surveyed the area. "Looks like Jo's coming our way. Hey, Jo!" She wore a fitted black jacket with faux fur on the cuffs and the hood. Looked terrific with her silver-gray hair.

"Hey, Sawyer clan. Hey, baby Josh." She came over and gave him a quick kiss on the cheek. "Is everybody ready to sing?"

"Depends on how you define the term," Pete said.

"Speak for yourself, big brother." Gage punched him lightly on the arm. "Last time I was at a karaoke bar, someone told me I sounded like Tim McGraw."

Wes grinned. "And how drunk was that person?"

"Doesn't really matter how any of us sound." Jo handed out the lyrics. "Not with all these people chiming in. Here's the drill. Deidre will stand on that stepladder at the front with one of those plane-parking batons. She'll be the choir director."

"Good choice." Pete looked at the songs. "Ha! *Grandma Got Run Over by a Reindeer.* Called it."

"It's a shortened version," Jo said. "We don't want this to run too long."

Gage held up his sheet of paper. "We're really going to play *Silent Night* on the kazoos?"

"Yes, we are," Jo said. "Your dad insists it'll be very pretty when a whole bunch of people play it nice and slow. Then we'll end with a quick chorus of *We Wish You a Merry Christmas* and we're done."

Ingrid took the paper Jo handed her. "Do Faith and Cody know we're out here?"

"Believe it or not, they don't," Jo said. "We've managed to keep it a secret."

Taryn glanced at Jo in surprise. "But can't they hear us?"

"Not when the house is closed up and the heat pump's on. Once we start, they'll hear us, though. Kendra, Quinn and Jim are up there with them. They used the excuse of bringing them dinner. They also smuggled a space heater out on the balcony so Faith and Noel can stay warm and cozy wrapped in a blanket in a deck chair."

Taryn nodded. "Good plan. This will be awesome."

"It will." Jo glanced around. "Everybody set, then?"

"I think we are," Pete said.

"Then I'll move on. It's almost time."

After she left, Taryn nudged him. "There's a woman with a video camera up on Deidre's stepladder filming the crowd. Bet she's the photographer they hired."

"She is," Roxanne said. "I heard Dad talking about getting her for tonight."

Taryn glanced at her. "Do you know her name?"

"He might have told me, but I've forgotten. I think she's relatively new in town. Are you looking for a photographer?"

"Yes, and if your dad hired her, that's good enough for me. I'll make sure I track her down and get her card."

"If you don't manage that, just call my dad."

"I will."

"And speaking of dear old dad, I hope he knows what he's doing." Gage shook his head. "*Silent Night* on the kazoo. Sounds like dicey city to me."

"We'll soon find out if it is or not," Wes said. "The photographer just came down the ladder and Deidre's going up."

"I'll bet she loves being the choir leader." Pete enjoyed the heck out of red-headed Deidre, the most flamboyant of the five members of the Whine and Cheese Club. As she stood on the top step of the ladder and studied the crowd, the rhinestones that trimmed her bright green coat sparkled in the light from the decorated trees.

She raised both hands, one holding the glowing orange wand. "Okay, everyone. On three," she called out. "One, two, *three!*"

The crowd launched into *Deck the Halls.* Shortly after that, the door to the balcony flew open and Cody barreled out, coatless and hatless. Calling Faith's name, he hurried back inside.

As the second verse of the song began, Faith came out all bundled up and supported by her dad and Cody. Kendra followed with the baby wrapped in a thick blanket, not a single part of that munchkin exposed to the cold air. Kendra moved close to the space heater and Faith eased onto a deck chair right next to it.

Last out the door was his dad, his broad grin telegraphing his excitement. His obvious happiness tugged at Pete's heart. The guy was in his element here. Thank heavens he'd decided to sell the Lazy S. Now he could spend the rest of his days with Kendra, surrounded by her kids, his kids, and the grandchildren.

When the first song ended, everyone on the balcony clapped and cheered except Kendra, who was smiling to beat the band with tears of joy glistening on her cheeks. *Grandma Got Run Over by a Reindeer* was next, which had everyone on the balcony laughing.

Then came *Jingle Bells.* Several people up front had brought sleigh bells and shook those somewhat in time to the tune. Roxanne was still holding Josh, and the little guy was rocking out, bouncing enthusiastically in her arms.

Pete didn't have to look at the lyrics for this one so he glanced over to check on Taryn. She was singing away, clearly into it. Then, without missing a beat, she looked at him and smiled.

Breathtaking. He returned her smile but he totally bungled the next line of the song. Seems he couldn't look at Taryn and sing at the same time. He recovered his mojo and finished up strong to work off the excess energy created by that smile.

"Everybody ready with your kazoos?" Deidre called from her perch.

Roxanne turned to him. "I'm afraid Josh will want mine if I try to play it. Which is okay, except if he drops it, then—"

"I have an idea." Pete held out his arms. "Maybe I can show him how to play it."

"Okay." She handed him over.

Pete settled Josh in the crook of his arm and took the kazoo out of his pocket. As everyone around them began playing the song, the little boy's eyes grew wide.

Pete leaned close and lowered his voice. "Want to try it?"

Josh reached for the kazoo.

"I'm gonna hold it, buddy, but you can play it." He positioned the kazoo so Josh could get his mouth around it. "Now hum. Like this." He demonstrated humming.

The kid was a quick study. He made that kazoo vibrate. It wasn't the right note, but who cared? He was part of the band.

Clearly he loved it. He got spit everywhere, but he made noise, by golly, and he kept at it as the strains of *Silent Night* filled the clearing.

Pete's chest warmed. He would never have guessed that all these adults—and one baby—playing *Silent Night* on kazoos would be so effective. It filled the tender lullaby with a sweet innocence that perfectly suited the mood of the song. His dad had been right.

As the last note died away, a peaceful silence fell upon the crowd, as if nobody wanted to break the spell. Then Deidre tapped her wand on the metal ladder, which was a signal to wrap it up with *We Wish You a Merry Christmas.*

Josh didn't want to give up the kazoo routine, so Pete let him continue humming and drooling through that number, too.

When it was over, shouts of *Merry Christmas* were exchanged between the folks on the balcony and people gathered in the clearing. The caroling was done, but Pete couldn't get Josh to give up the kazoo. He'd clamped down on it with his teeth.

"Hey, buddy, I need that back, okay?" Pete tried to wiggle it free, but the little boy had amazing strength in his jaw. "Guess I'd better get your mom and dad to help with this."

He glanced around for Taryn and found her a few feet away talking with the photographer. Excellent. He didn't want to interrupt that conversation so he headed over toward Gage and Emma.

"That was awesome," Emma said.

"It was." Pete kept a firm grip on the kazoo while Josh did the same. "I had no idea it would sound that good."

"I don't mean the caroling. I meant you and Josh. You let him participate. It was adorable. Thank you."

"Yeah," Gage said. "You're a hell of an uncle, bro. He was drooling all over the place. Not everybody would put up with that."

"Ah, what's a little spit between friends? But I might have created a problem. He doesn't want to give it up. He's clamped his teeth around it. I was afraid to pull too hard in case I'd hurt him."

"I can fix this." Emma went around behind Gage and dug into the backpack he was wearing. "Hey, Josh, want a cookie?"

The little boy immediately lost interest in the kazoo and Pete. He went straight into Emma's arms.

Pete reached in his back pocket for his bandanna and wiped off the very wet kazoo.

"Gonna keep it?"

He glanced at Gage, who had a teasing light in his eyes. "Thought I would for old time's sake. Why?"

Gage pulled a yellow one out of his jacket pocket. "Want to trade?"

"Because mine's green?"

"No, because it has Josh's teeth marks on it. It would be a great souvenir of tonight and his first try at playing a kazoo." He hesitated. "But you might want it for the same reason."

"It's yours." He swapped with Gage. "That's a very cool kid you've got there, bro."

"Yes, he is." He glanced at Emma, who was brushing cookie crumbs off Josh's snowsuit. "I'm a lucky man in so many ways."

"I agree."

Gage stepped closer and lowered his voice. "Listen, it's probably none of my business, but do I sense a little something happening between you and Taryn?"

"Uh, no, not really."

"Hm." Gage studied him. Then he reached out and squeezed his shoulder. "Play the long game, bro. It's working for me."

"Thanks for the advice." He wouldn't go into it with Gage, especially right now, but there was no game, long or short. He wanted what was best for Taryn. Near as he could tell, getting chummy with him didn't fit in that category.

6

Talk about adorable. Pete helping Josh play the kazoo had captured Taryn's attention so completely that she'd stopped playing to watch. The image would stay with her a long time.

She was going to tell him so, but then she spotted the photographer nearby and walked over to introduce herself. Turned out the woman's name was Caitlin Dempsey and she'd lived in Eagles Nest less than a year. The crowd started to move as she and Caitlin were discussing Crimson Clouds so they walked down the hill together.

Taryn finally rejoined Pete and his family during the outdoor dinner, where the number of people, the bonfire and a cup of hot coffee kept her warm. Conversation was free-wheeling and hilarious, but it wasn't the time for a private word with Pete.

Once they were on their way back to her ranch, he asked what she'd learned about the photographer.

"She's great. Like me, she missed the Fourth of July celebration because she was visiting family, but she's already promised the town council she'll stay in Eagles Nest for the next one and create a documentary-style video of the day. I gather she's made a name for herself in a very short time."

"Did you set a date for her to come out?"

"Not yet, but I have an idea. It's ambitious, though."

"Hit me. I like ambitious ideas."

"I've noticed." She was slightly out of breath and more aware of him than she wanted to be. *Shake it off, girl.* She cleared her throat. "After seeing how appealing Wild Creek looks decorated, I've decided I'd be missing an opportunity if I don't offer a special holiday package for Christmas next winter."

He nodded. "I think it would be popular."

"Me, too, and I want to advertise it now while people are involved in this year's celebration. Which means I need a visual."

"I'm guessing you want to put up some lights."

"If you'll help me. And I'm hoping Caitlin's available to take some video and stills for the website."

"When?"

"Day after tomorrow. If she came in the late afternoon, she could get some daylight shots and some evening ones."

"Do you have lights?"

"I have a stash I bought in November, just in case I wanted to decorate the front porch and the two trees in the yard, maybe the roofline of the barn."

"That should be doable."

"But I'd also love to put lights in some of the bigger trees in that grove near the barn."

"Whoa."

"Not on the scale of Wild Creek, obviously. Maybe only three or four trees. I'd need a larger size of lights than what I have, though."

"You'd have to run a conduit out there and get a bucket truck to install the lights."

"Is a bucket truck the kind with a crane thing on the back?"

"Yep."

"Then that's what I'd need. Lighting the big trees might not work out, at least for this year. For one thing, getting an electrician on short notice—"

"I could do it."

"You could?"

"Dad taught me how to wire something like that. We had similar lighting at the Lazy S for Christmas. My guess is he was the mastermind behind the lights in the trees at Wild Creek. I've also operated a bucket truck."

"Are you saying we might actually be able to pull this off?"

"Maybe, assuming we can get the bigger lights and reserve a bucket truck. If not, we can still decorate the ranch house, the yard and maybe the barn."

"So you're in?"

"I'm in." He flashed her a smile.

And she went all fizzy inside. Not a good sign. "Awesome. I'll text Caitlin right now." She pulled out her phone and sent a quick message. "She might not answer until tomorrow."

"What if she's not available? Do you still want to do it?"

"Yes, but I hope she is. I'll end up with something much more professional. I talked with her about how she filmed the lights in the trees. It takes more skill and better equipment than I have."

"Then let's hope she's free. And I'm glad going over there inspired you to come up with this."

"It's been an amazing night. Which reminds me, Josh was so cute with that kazoo. You did a great job with him."

A smile dented his cheek. "I'm crazy about that little booger. I can't wait to see how he reacts to Christmas. Last year he would have been too young to get much out of it, but now he should have a pretty good idea of what's going on."

"Do you think Gage and Emma will take him to see Santa? I assume there's a Santa for the kids to visit somewhere in town, although I didn't think to ask about it."

"Oh, yeah, there is. Hank, the guy who fills in at the soda fountain on Sundays, does the Santa thing at Pills and Pop."

"When?"

"He was there last Saturday afternoon from one to four and he'll do it again this Saturday. Ellie Mae Stockton dresses up as Mrs. Claus and gives each kid a little stuffed toy when they leave."

"How do you know all this?"

"My dad made it a point to find out. Then he asked Emma if she'd be willing to wait and take Josh to see Santa when she came down here."

"I'm sure she said yes. Kendra and Quinn will be there with their phones at the ready."

"I have a hunch most of Josh's fan club will show up. I was planning to ask for the afternoon off so I can go."

"Of course! I'd like to watch, too."

"Great. We can ride in together, then." He checked for traffic and passed a slow-moving truck ahead of them. "Are you going to the talent show at the GG that night?"

"I wouldn't miss it."

"Unless you've made other plans, want to go with me?"

Oh. She hadn't made other plans. No point in turning him down after she'd just invited herself along to watch Josh sitting on Santa's lap. "I'd like that."

"Excellent. We can—"

"There's my phone." She read the text. "Woo-hoo! She can do it!" Typing quickly, she confirmed the time with Caitlin. "She wants to know if she'll be doing any interior shots. And me with no decorations up yet."

"Do you have any for inside?"

"I have all I need for the tree. Brought it from San Francisco, plus a few other things, like a sleigh and reindeer, a cute Santa and Mrs. Claus, a few holiday-themed pillows. I've been picking up pinecones since September, so I have a whole bag of those. And weather-resistant red ribbon. Lots of that. But no tree. I plan to cut my own, but I haven't done it."

"We might have time to cut one."

"Then I'll tell her to come prepared to shoot the interior just in case." She typed her reply. "Now I'm getting excited. Last time I was in town, I noticed a decorative sleigh outside the hardware store. It was about half the size of a functional one but it would look cool in the yard. Could be gone by now."

"I think it's still there. First order of business is checking on the bucket truck. The equipment rental place opens early. I'll make that call first thing in the morning."

"Good. I'll get out all the lights I already have before I go to bed tonight. And ribbon and other stuff. First thing in the morning, I'll do some measuring in the yard and create a rough schematic."

"That'll help." He pulled up in front of her house, shut off the engine and hopped out so he could open her door.

When she'd first hired him and they'd started running errands together, she'd mentioned that she didn't expect him to help her out of his truck every time. He'd explained that he couldn't operate any other way. He'd been trained from a young age to open doors for women and it was completely ingrained at this point.

She'd accepted that and he'd been opening doors for her ever since. She'd come to enjoy it. Except their dynamic had changed. It wasn't a simple courtesy anymore.

Placing her hand in his firm grip, even though she was wearing her knit gloves, was like touching a live wire. Her pulse refused to behave.

"I'll walk you to the door."

"That's not really necess—"

"It is to me. When I bring a lady home after dark, I walk her to the door." He let go of her hand, though.

"I guess you've never brought me home after dark."

"That would be a fact." He walked beside her up to the porch. "This is the first time we've spent an evening together. And for the record, I had fun."

"So did I." She climbed the steps and walked to the front door. Sure did feel like the end of a date. She turned to him. "Thank you for taking me over there tonight. What a special event. I'm glad I was part of it."

"I am, too." He gazed at her, his hands in the pockets of his jacket, the porch light reflecting in his gray eyes. "Goodnight, Taryn."

The way he said her name was different from the way he used to say it. She responded in a crisp, no-nonsense tone. "Goodnight, Pete. Thanks again." She gave him a quick smile and opened the door.

"See you first thing in the morning."

Not so long from now. "See you then." She walked into the house, shut the door and leaned against it with a sigh.

She'd started this with her flirty comment about the honeymoon bed. She'd worked hard to move past that little slip, but awareness crackled in the air whenever she was alone with him. Clearly he felt it, too.

Could be just a temporary crush, something that would wear off if she ignored it. That would be a blessing.

7

The temperature was in the teens when Pete pulled up in front of Taryn's house the next morning, but she was outside with a clipboard and a metal tape measure. She wore her parka with the hood up and a scarf tied around her neck, plus fingerless gloves so she could write. With a quick wave, she went back to studying the front yard.

He'd never looked at it with an eye to Christmas lights, but it had possibilities. A picturesque rail fence created a break between the circular drive and the flagstone path leading up to the porch. A pair of full, well-shaped blue spruces sat on either side of the path.

He climbed down, buttoned his jacket and turned up the collar. He admired her grit, coming out at first light to create a schematic for them to work from. This project would have been so much easier to plan in September, but she hadn't been thinking about Christmas then. She'd been worried about whether the initial four cabins would be finished before the first snow.

They had been. Although Eagles Nest had seen a couple of snowstorms, they'd been mild and a warm spell in early December had melted everything but small patches in deep shade. The temperature today could get up in the high thirties, maybe even low forties, decent weather for this venture.

Tugging on his leather gloves, he walked over to where she'd crouched next to the fence. "I reserved us a bucket truck. I'll pick it up first thing in the morning."

"Yay!" She stood and faced him. "That's one piece of the puzzle." As usual first thing in the morning, her cheeks were pink from the cold and her lips were pale.

She'd never worn makeup for working in the barn. She'd announced early on that she didn't think the horses cared. He'd promised not to wear makeup, either, which had made her laugh.

He gestured toward the fence. "I take it you'd like to light this?"

"Yes, definitely. There's an outlet on the porch." She turned the clipboard so he could see it. "Maybe you could run a line from there down here." Her breath condensed in the frigid air.

"Shouldn't take too long. That'll give you the option of lighting the porch, the fence and both trees. What else?"

"I want to do the roofline of the barn and maybe a lighted wreath over the double doors, if the hardware store still has any. The barn's loaded with outlets, so that's only a matter of getting everything up. No extra wiring needed."

"I agree."

"Same thing with the cabin we put the furniture in yesterday. Since that's the one you can see from here, I'd like to do some lights on the outside of it."

"Do you have enough for all that?"

"Believe it or not, I do. I tend to overbuy when I get Christmas lights. But I didn't get any that are the right size to show up on those tall trees in the grove. Fingers crossed that the hardware store has a supply of them. They might not since it's this close to Christmas."

"If they don't, I'll bet Caitlin can work with what we put up."

"I'm sure, but let's feed and turn out the horses as quickly as we can. Then maybe we can make it into town before the store opens."

"Right." He waited while she took the clipboard and tape measure up to the porch. Her enthusiasm for a new project was part of what he liked about the job. His skills were helping her build her dream.

She came back minus her scarf since she wouldn't be needing it in the barn. "I'm so glad we're tackling this project. I already have an image in my head of how beautiful it will look."

"Me, too." He fell into step beside her. "Especially after last night. They created a fairyland out there."

"Have you talked to anyone? Any feedback on how baby Noel is doing?"

"I had a quick conversation with my dad this morning and she's doing great. Faith and Cody were so touched by the caroling. And totally surprised."

"They didn't suspect anything when a bucket truck showed up in their meadow?"

"Oh, they knew Kendra and my dad were installing the lights to celebrate the baby's birth. Cody and his brothers helped light those trees. But the hundred-plus crowd coming out to sing to them—that was the shocker."

"What a brainstorm, too. Who thought of it?"

"Dad said the idea came out of a Whine and Cheese Club gathering." He opened the barn doors. "Vino was involved. When those five women get together, no telling what they'll decide to do."

"Isn't that the truth. Okay. Let's get cracking."

* * *

Creating the image Taryn carried in her head was exactly the kind of challenge Pete thrived on. Once the horses were taken care of, they hopped in his truck and headed for town. Even at this early hour, Main Street was busy. "Visualize a parking space opening up, okay?" He scanned the area in front of the hardware store.

"Someone's pulling out."

"So they are." He put on his blinker and waited. "Looks like your sleigh is sitting right out front waiting for you."

"Maybe not. There's a Sold sign on it."

"Well, damn. I didn't see that." He eased into the parking space and shut off the motor. "Maybe they have another one." Putting on his hat, he hurried around to let her out.

"It's okay if it's gone," she said as he opened her door. "I'm not all that surprised."

"Let's go see if they have one in the back."

But when they got inside, Ira, the store's owner, said he'd only ordered one. "I was beginning to think nobody would buy it and I'd have to put it away until next year." He shoved his glasses to the top of his bald head. "Then Virginia Bennett decided she needed it for that wedding venue of hers and called me five minutes ago with her credit card number. Badger should be along to pick it up any time, now."

Pete nudged back his hat. "Why is Badger coming to get it?"

"Oh, you know Badger." Ira chuckled. "He loves to help out, especially when it comes to his future mother-in-law."

"Are Badger and Hayley officially engaged? I hadn't heard that."

"I don't know that it's official yet, but everyone's positive they'll end up together. Anyway, to make a long story short, I'm afraid the sleigh is taken."

Pete glanced at Taryn. "I guess you could order a sleigh like that one and have it for next year."

"I will. We can manage without it."

"Maybe we could engineer something else as a focal point for the yard." He had no idea what, though. The sleigh, especially with lights on it, would have been perfect. "I'll think about it while we're getting the other stuff. Maybe we'll—"

"And here comes Badger," Ira said. "Right on time."

"Hey, y'all." Badger was all smiles, as usual. "Pete, my man, could I borrow you for a few minutes? I could use a hand loadin' that little sleigh out front."

"I can, but let me ask you something. Could Virginia wait on that sleigh? Maybe get it after Christmas?"

"No sir. She needs it ASAP. She has three Christmas-themed weddin' ceremonies comin' up, startin' with one tonight."

"Okay, then never mind."

"Why are you askin'?"

"We're setting up to do a photo shoot at the ranch tomorrow. Taryn was hoping to use that sleigh as a prop in her yard. Maybe add some greenery and lights. I thought if Virginia didn't need it right away, we could borrow it for a little while."

"Unfortunately she's expectin' me to bring it over in the next thirty minutes." He gazed at Taryn. "How 'bout an alternative?"

"Oh, absolutely," she said. "Don't worry about it. I'm sure we'll think of something."

"I'm sure you will, too, but I'll feel a whole lot better drivin' off with that sleigh if I know you've latched onto a new concept for your yard. I'll help y'all." He crossed his arms and surveyed the store.

Taryn smiled. "That's sweet, but you need to deliver—"

"Aha! What about that thingamajig?" He pointed to a green metal garden arch. "Couldn't you shove pine branches in that, then add some ribbons and lights? That could be real pretty."

"That's actually a good possibility." Taryn gazed at the arch. "It could sit at the entrance to the walkway between the two sections of rail fence. We were going to decorate the fence anyway."

"I just got another idea." Pete turned to Ira. "I'll bet you have wagon wheels in the back."

"I do. Several sizes."

"We could get two big ones, weave greenery and ribbon through the spokes, add lights and prop them against the fence on each side of the arch."

"There you go." Badger glanced over at Taryn. "I'm thinkin' that'll do the trick." He lifted his eyebrows. "How 'bout you?"

"I love it. Wonderful alternative."

"Alrighty, then. Now I'll be takin' that sleigh with a clear conscience."

"Come on," Pete said. "I'll help you load 'er up."

"That'll be great."

"While you're doing that," Taryn said, "I'll check the light situation."

"Great. See you in a bit." Pete moved toward the door.

Badger started after him, but turned back. "Will you be attendin' the talent show, Miss Taryn?"

"I'll be there. Can't wait."

"You'll love it." He smiled and tipped his hat. "See you Saturday night."

"Looking forward to it."

Badger followed Pete out the door. "She's nice. I like her."

"I do, too."

"I can tell."

"It's not what you're thinking."

"But you wish it could be."

Pete sighed. Evidently he appeared to need help in this area. Gage had felt the urge to give him a tip last night and now Badger seemed to be working up to the same thing. "Look, if you're about to give me advice, I'm—"

"Nope, nope." Badger held up both hands. "Just makin' an observation."

"Okay."

"Am I right?"

"We'd better load this sleigh. Your future mother-in-law's waiting."

He grinned. "I'm right."

8

Taryn bought every strand of large white lights Ira had, including all the ones in the storeroom. She found a lighted wreath to go over the barn door, too. Pete picked up the electric supplies he needed and they loaded everything in the truck.

She pulled out her phone. "Have you tried the new text ordering system for Pie in the Sky?"

"Can't say I have."

"It's efficient. If I text an order for two coffees to go, they'll be ready in about five minutes. Want one?"

"Sure, why not."

"And a Christmas sugar cookie?"

He laughed. "Twist my arm."

"I'm getting a Candy Cane Latte. Do you want one of those or an Epic Eggnog Espresso?"

"The espresso, please. And make it a double shot."

"I just changed my mind. I'm getting that, too. Might as well give myself some extra caffeine so I can power through this job."

"That was my thought."

"Do you want a wreath cookie or a tree cookie?"

"I seem to remember a Santa and a snowman, too."

"Yes, but there's something so wrong about chomping down on Santa and Frosty. I never get those."

He grinned. "And you'd prefer I didn't?"

"Yes, I would."

"A wreath's fine."

"Good choice." She sent in the order and fifteen minutes later they were on the road to Crimson Clouds as they sipped their espressos and ate wreath-shaped cookies.

Eagerness for the project carried her through the rest of what became a long day of constant effort, interrupted only by a fifteen-minute lunch break of hastily made sandwiches. By the time the light began to fade, the porch and yard were finished. Pete had used an extension ladder to string lights along the roofline of the barn and hang the lighted wreath. He'd also installed a conduit from the barn to the grove of trees.

She was ready to call it a day, but first she wanted to sit with him and plan their next steps. She made a pot of coffee and they settled on the front porch steps with steaming mugs. The lights were on, but it wasn't dark enough yet for them to show up well.

She took a sip from her mug. "So, tomorrow we'll do the grove of trees and the one cabin."

He nodded. "I have to have the truck back by four but that should give us plenty of time for the trees. What about your Christmas tree?"

"It's still in the forest." She'd concentrated so hard on the outside she'd forgotten that she'd mentioned decorating a tree.

"If you're not too bushed, we should have enough light to cut one if we go as soon as we finish our coffee."

"Aren't you tired? We've been going nonstop since you arrived this morning."

"I'm a little tired, but cutting the tree won't take long and decorating it is the fun part."

"Are you offering to help me?"

"Well, yeah, unless you don't want me to."

"I'd appreciate the help, but don't you have things to do at home?"

He shrugged. "Nothing critical. I can text Dad and ask him to feed Clifford. I'm not trying to push you into getting the tree, but if you had it up and a fire going when Caitlin gets here, and maybe a couple of the Christmas things you mentioned like pillows and such, she could shoot in there, too."

"I guess it makes sense to have her take as many pictures as possible once she's here." She gazed at him. "But if you stay to help me with the tree, I'll need to feed us both, and I—"

"I'm not picky. Whatever you usually have is fine."

"I'm not so sure. I usually have wine, a few slices of cheese, a handful or two of nuts, maybe some crackers if I'm feeling wild and crazy. And olives. I have some of those in the fridge."

"That's all you eat for dinner?"

His shocked tone made her laugh. "I've never been into cooking. I make myself breakfast, and lunch is usually sandwiches or soup, as you've probably noticed. I don't have anything in the pantry or the fridge that qualifies as a proper dinner entrée. Not my thing."

"Okay, I'll admit those few little munchies won't do it for me. Do you have any eggs?"

"Yes."

"Is there any of that bread left?"

"I have plenty of bread. I always have toast in the morning."

"How about syrup? Oh, and milk. I'll need sugar, too."

"I have a bag of sugar. I also have cream for my coffee."

"Cream will work even better, but I don't want to leave you without any for tomorrow morning."

"No worries. I have plenty. As for the syrup, let me think. You know, I do have some maple syrup that somebody gave me a while ago. Never opened it. And I think I've figured out what's on the menu for tonight."

"I'll make you the best French toast you've ever had."

"Yum! French toast for dinner. How decadent. I can't wait."

"Then let's go get that tree." He finished his coffee and stood. "Assuming you have a saw."

"I do. A bow saw."

"Perfect."

"Ira told me so when I bought it." She poured the rest of her coffee in the flower bed next to the steps. "I'll get it."

"Did you plan to cut your own tree?"

"I did, although now that you're here to help, I'll choose a bigger one."

He grinned. "I see."

"Be right back." She carried both mugs into the house, took the saw out of the laundry room where she kept her tools, and returned to the front porch.

"Do you know where you want to look?"

"Yep. We'll go a little beyond that grove of trees where you'll be stringing lights tomorrow. There are several potential trees I've looked at." She held out the saw.

"Oh, no." He backed away. "Your saw, your tree. I'm just the muscle that allows you to get a bigger tree, but you're in charge of this operation."

She smiled. "Okay, but if you'd hold it for a minute I want to zip my parka and put on my gloves."

"Sure thing."

"Now I'm ready." She took the saw and started off. "I feel like a real ranch woman, doing this."

"You are a real ranch woman."

She glanced at him. "I suppose I am, now that you mention it. I've learned a lot, most of it thanks to you."

"It's been a pleasure. I'll admit when you hired me I didn't expect you'd work alongside me the way you have."

"I had a professor I adored who told his students to learn as much about the property as possible, do many of the jobs, get familiar with what goes on."

"You could have watched me muck out stalls, though. You didn't have to get in there and do it."

"I think I do have to get in there and do it. Besides, it's good exercise and it...I dunno...helps me think."

"And that's what any true ranch woman would say. Or cowboy. That particular job has a way of putting life into perspective."

"I know! In fact, when the guests start arriving, I might not have the time to muck out stalls. Then what?"

"Guess you'll have to find a substitute."

"I don't know what that would be." She pointed to a path through the trees. "Through here. We'll have to go single file."

"Ladies first."

She walked ahead of him on the path that someone had once cleared but was overgrown, now. "The only time I'll have to myself once the guests arrive will be after eight in the evening, when they're on their own. That's not when I should be mucking out stalls."

"No, guess not. That's a morning chore." He sounded amused.

"I know it sounds ridiculous, but my time in the stable with the horses has become so precious to me."

"You could go down and hang out with them in the evening, give Honey Butter a rubdown. He'd love that."

"Good idea. Got any more where that came from?"

His soft chuckle was followed by an even softer *no.*

A delicious shiver traveled down her spine. Damn his hide, he was thinking about sex. She'd swear to it. It was certainly an activity she could enjoy after eight in the evening, and one that would provide exercise and often a new perspective if you had the right partner.

She had no doubt he could give her a new perspective and he very well could be the right partner...at the wrong time. She was about to launch a business. He was a key player.

The thick stand of trees opened onto a small meadow. Twilight was upon them, but she was able to pinpoint the group of evergreens she'd identified as good prospects. "Over here."

"I see them. Nice shapes."

She started toward them. "I'd zeroed in on the one on the far left, but the one on the far right would fit my living room better."

"It's a little too tall for your ceiling."

"You think? It looks perfect to me."

"They always look smaller when they're outside."

She laughed. "Yeah, okay, I've seen *Christmas Vacation.* Maybe the shorter one's better."

"But the shape isn't as good. We could cut the other one about three feet up the trunk. That could potentially preserve the tree. If what I've read is correct, it'll grow back."

"No kidding? That would be fantastic."

"It's worth a shot, and there's even a logical place about three feet up where the branches aren't as thick."

"I see where you're talking about. Should I just get in there and start cutting?"

"Go for it. I'd start on this side."

Taking a deep breath, she placed the blade against the tree trunk and went to work. After about a minute she paused to unzip her jacket. "This isn't all that easy, is it?"

"You're doing great. Keep going. When you get about halfway, stop."

"Then you'll take over?"

"Only if you want me to."

Her arms were aching and she was breathing hard, but she was cutting her own Christmas tree. "I want to finish it."

"Then when you get halfway, you need to go around and work from the opposite side."

"Okay." She stopped at the point he'd recommended and stood back. "It'll look gorgeous in my living room."

"Yes, it will."

Something in his tone made her glance at him. In the soft twilight, his expression appeared tender, even slightly besotted. But she could be wrong. Darkness was closing in. "I'd better finish up while I can still see what I'm doing." She walked around the tree and started on the other side. Maybe she was getting the hang of it, because the sawing went faster.

"Slow down a little, you're almost there…move away. It should fall in my direction, but—there it goes!"

With a sharp crack, the top three-quarters of the tree toppled to the ground with a loud thump.

"I did it!" She hurried around to the other side. "I cut my own Christmas tree!"

"Congratulations."

This time there was no doubt about the warmth of his gaze. She was standing right next to him. Couldn't miss it even in the dim light. Made her tingle all over.

She swallowed. "We should head back."

"Yep." He cleared his throat. "I'll take the tree."

She glanced at it. Ginormous. Pete was a strong guy, but still… "Maybe you could just drag it along the—"

"Don't want to risk breaking off branches." Crouching down, he got his shoulder under the main part of the trunk and stood. "Let's go."

She stared at him for a moment, transfixed by the manly image of him balancing that huge tree on his shoulder. "I'll lead the way." She pulled her phone out of her pocket and activated the flashlight app. "This will help. Holler if I'm going too fast."

"I will."

She kept her light trained on the ground as she navigated the path, calling out warnings about roots and depressions that might trip him.

As she neared the end, her breath caught. "Pete, the lights are gorgeous."

"I can see them. Not the whole thing from here, but—"

"So pretty!" The closer she came to the house, the better her view. "Can you put down the tree and come look?" She hurried toward the driveway.

"Sure. Be right there." Changing direction, he walked over to the side of the house and leaned the tree against it.

"Oh, man, it's so great! Amazing!" She stood in the driveway, backing up to get the full effect. "The arch and the wagon wheels work so well. I think I like that better than the sleigh idea."

Pete came over to stand beside her. "Yeah. It turned out really nice."

"Thank you for going along with my spur-of-the-moment plan to do all this decorating." Just thanking him seemed inadequate. Seemed like she should do something more, like hug him. Ah, no. Bad idea. She let out a breath. "We make a great team."

"Uh, huh."

Amazing how much depth of emotion he conveyed in two measly syllables. It warmed her all the way to her toes.

9

Pete's resistance to Taryn was wearing dangerously thin, but he figured he had enough willpower left to fix the French toast he'd promised and help her trim the tree. Then he'd hightail it outta there before he blew the whole program by kissing her.

While she went in search of her tree stand, he hauled the pine up on the porch and waited for her signal that the stand was in place. Getting chilly out here. Would she make a fire? Eating French toast in front of the fire would be nice. Maybe too nice...

She opened the door. "It's set up. You can bring it in."

He backed the tree in so the branches would fold toward the trunk and make it through the door.

"It smells wonderful."

"Sure does. To me, Christmas doesn't start until you bring in the sweet-smelling tree."

"I absolutely agree with you."

"Where's it going?"

"Over in that corner." She pointed to it. "Should be far enough away from the fireplace so it won't be a hazard, but Caitlin will be able to get a shot of both the fireplace and the tree."

"Good choice. Could you get down on the floor and guide me as I put it in the stand? It's so bushy I can't see what I'm doing."

"Gotcha." She dropped to her hands and knees, peered under the tree and called out directions. "That's great, right there. You're centered."

He shoved the tree onto the metal spike. "I'll steady it while you tighten the screws."

"I'm on it." She crawled around him, brushing against his legs as she secured the tree in the stand.

All this proximity was torture, but he was the doofus who'd suggested getting the tree and decorating it tonight. Setting up a Christmas tree required working closely together. He hadn't factored that in.

"It should be solid. You can let go."

He slowly released his hold on the trunk and the tree stayed put. Then he backed away. "It has a great shape. No bad side."

Getting to her feet, she brushed off her hands. "I didn't see any when I was cutting it. I'll get the lights and ornaments."

"Need help?"

"Nope." She hurried down the hall. "Got everything packed in one box and it's light."

He unbuttoned his jacket and hung it on a row of hooks she had by the door. Put his hat on another one.

"Here we go." She set the box on the floor next to the tree and opened the flaps. "I think we need something to drink and a few munchies to get us through until it's French toast time. Want a beer?"

"Love one. Thanks." It wasn't the first time he'd shared a beer with her, but they hadn't done it often. They'd usually opened a couple of bottles to toast a new horse in the barn. And they'd celebrated with a beer after each of the cabins had been finished.

She came out of the kitchen with two long necks dangling from one hand and an open package of potato chips in the other. "We have so many fun things to toast that I don't know which to choose. There's Noel Lorraine, and the decision to offer a Christmas vacation package, and the beautiful lights, and—"

"I know what to toast." He took the bottle she handed him. "To your first Christmas in Eagles Nest."

"That's a good toast." She touched her bottle to his. "To my first Christmas in Eagles Nest. And yours." She took a long swallow and sighed. "Just think. If my folks hadn't made reservations for a Dickens Christmas in London, I'd be in San Francisco right now."

"Do you miss them?"

"A little. It seems weird since we've never been apart for Christmas. But that was a foregone conclusion even before the divorce. They wanted us to go with them, but my ex wasn't interested." She held out the chips. "Want some?"

"Sure." He took a few out of the bag.

She set it on the coffee table and pulled out a handful for herself. "After we filed for divorce my parents were all set to spend a ton of money to add me to their travel plans, but I'd already negotiated with my ex to get this place as part of our settlement and I was eager to plunge into my guest ranch idea. So here I am." She popped a chip into her mouth.

"I don't think you ever told me why you and your ex bought the property."

"It was mostly my idea. I've always liked the idea of investing in real estate. It was supposed to be an investment and a getaway for us, but a guest ranch was in the back of my mind from the beginning."

"Why?"

"The romance of it." She ate another chip.

"Excuse me?"

"In my hospitality classes we studied all kinds of scenarios—hotels, inns, cruise ships, B&Bs, and guest ranches. A ranch was completely out of my experience and it sounded exotic, romantic, exciting."

"What's your take on it now that you've dealt with the nitty-gritty?"

"Kind of the same."

"Hm." He gazed at her. "Well, if you haven't been scared off by the work you've done so far, I expect you'll end up sticking around."

"I expect I will." She set her beer on the coffee table and crouched next to the box. "Oh, wow, we get to string more lights! I'll bet you're excited."

"Matter of fact, I am." He left his beer next to hers. "These are colored."

"That they are." She reached in the box and brought out two neat bundles of lights. "When it comes to the tree inside, I'm all about the colored lights." After plugging in each set to test it, she handed him one. "And look at that. I don't need to haul out a stepstool. You can reach the top of this sucker."

"Just barely. I don't know if two strands will be enough."

"That's okay. I have a third one in there if it's not. Here, I'll get behind the tree and we can pass the strand back and forth."

"Just about to suggest that." The job went quickly, as it usually did when he worked with Taryn. Except ever since yesterday he experienced a little jolt of pleasure every time his hand touched hers. "By the way, the lights on those big pines won't be going around the tree."

She laughed. "They won't?"

"Not unless one of us sprouts wings during the night."

"I've always wished I could fly."

"Want to come up in the bucket with me tomorrow when I do those trees? It's not exactly flying, but you'd get a bird's-eye view."

"I would *love* to go up in the bucket. I didn't think of that option. What fun."

He should have known she'd want to. "Be sure and bundle up. It'll be colder up there, especially if there's a breeze."

"I can take it. All right, I'm plugging in the lights. Eyeball it and see how it looks." She came out from behind the tree.

"Hold still. You have a piece of a pine branch in your hair." Walking over, he gently disentangled it. He'd never touched her hair before and it took great self-control not to run his fingers through those silky waves.

"Thanks." She sounded breathless and she moved away quickly. "Lights look perfect to me! It's ornament time!"

He glanced at the segmented boxes she laid out on the coffee table. No two ornaments were alike. "Looks like these were collected one at a time."

"Yep. They were all on the big family tree until I got married." She hung a fabric star with her name embroidered on it. "Then my folks insisted I take them." She glanced at him. "You can hang some if you want."

"I'm worried I'll drop an heirloom."

"Nah, I trust you."

"Alrighty, then." He joined her in the familiar ritual and as a bonus, he learned more about her past because each ornament had a story.

Gradually, sipping beer and eating chips along the way, they emptied the boxes. When they'd finished, he glanced at her. "If your folks gave you all these, wasn't their tree a little bare?"

"It would have been, but they went with a smaller tree. We used to get a humongous one. They plan to collect more ornaments and I'm sure they'll buy a bunch in London. They'll have a humongous tree again in no time."

"I hope I get to meet your folks one day. They sound like happy people."

"They are, and I'm sure you will meet them. They would have been over to visit before now, except I asked them to hold off until I'd pulled the place together."

"Then they should be showing up soon."

"It's close." Taking a deep red ribbon out of the box, she created a zigzag pattern across the front half of the tree. "And we're done! I can almost taste that French toast. I'll get you started in the kitchen and then I'll build a fire."

"Can we eat in front of it?"

"That was my plan. The coffee table can be raised to dining table height."

"I didn't know that." But why would he? He'd never spent an evening in her house. Or sat on her sofa, if it came to that.

For months he'd worked side-by-side with her, often sharing a cup of coffee and an occasional beer. He'd eaten lunch with her many times, either at the ranch or in town. But through all that he'd still been the hired hand who'd gone home every day after the horses had been fed.

She headed into the kitchen. "I have an electric griddle if that's—"

"Exactly what I like to work with. A much faster way to accomplish it than a frying pan."

"Then here's that." She took it out of a cupboard. "And a bowl, and a whisk—eggs, cream and butter in the fridge..." She turned to him. "What else?"

"Vanilla and cinnamon."

She got a bottle of vanilla from another cupboard and cinnamon from her spice rack. "Done and done."

"Then I'm all set. I'm thinking we'll want coffee with this."

"Yeah. Beer and French toast. Blech." She made a face. "I'll start the coffee."

"Okay." While she measured out the beans and dumped them in the grinder, he took what he needed from the fridge. They moved around the kitchen easily, as if they were used to operating together in a kitchen even though they'd never done it before. Made sense. They'd been sharing barn duties for months.

Once Taryn had understood the barn routine and had become comfortable with the tasks, she'd performed them with an admirable efficiency of movement. That was also his strong suit, and their morning and evening chores had become almost like a dance. He'd never mentioned that to her. Hadn't seemed appropriate.

Besides, he wasn't given to saying stuff like that. He wasn't a flowery speech sort of guy. Telling a woman that working with her in the barn was as effortless as dancing...well, he could guarantee it wouldn't come out right. Better to keep that concept to himself.

She left the kitchen to go build a fire and he threw himself into making the best damn French toast of his life. He didn't have a large repertoire, only two or three things, really, but what he could make was food for the gods.

His secret was dipping the bread in the bowl, arranging all the pieces on the skillet and spooning the rest of the mixture on each individual piece. Then they puffed up like nobody's business.

If he were at home, he wouldn't bother getting fancy, but because he wanted to impress Taryn, he cut the slices in half diagonally before dipping them. They looked better on the plate that way.

"Smells delicious." She came back into the kitchen to get silverware, placemats and napkins.

"So does the fire. Nothing like cedar."

"My favorite. How soon before we eat?"

"Less than five minutes."

"Good. I'm starving." She left with their utensils.

She had more than one set of plates so he chose the ones with a turquoise center and a beige rim decorated with Native American symbols. Then he found a small pan and poured the syrup into it. Might as well do this right. He set the pan on the burner and turned it on low. Then he went back to the cupboard where he'd found the plates and took out a ceramic pitcher that matched.

"I see you found my favorite plates."

He glanced up. "I can see why they would be. If you were going to serve someone breakfast in that bed we put together, these would be the ones to use." The words had popped right out. He hadn't meant them to be suggestive.

But her cheeks turned pink. "I guess they would. Are you ready for me to pour the coffee?"

"Yes, ma'am. I'll be in with the food in two shakes of a lamb's tail."

She took out mugs that matched the plates, filled them and carried them into the living room.

The French toast was the exact shade he'd been going for and the slices looked festive laid across the plates in a neat row. Some strawberries tucked along the edges would look good, but that was a summertime garnish.

He poured the syrup into the pitcher, made sure everything was turned off, and balanced both plates on one arm so he could carry the syrup in his other hand.

Taryn had taken a seat on the sofa, and she turned and smiled when he came in. "Hey, now. Somebody's had experience as a waiter."

"Earned some extra cash that way when I was in high school." He put down the pitcher before setting her plate in front of her. "Isn't the table a little too far away?"

"Yep. There are wheels cleverly disguised in the legs. Once you sit down we'll pull it forward."

"That's quite a versatile piece of furniture."

"When you work in hotel management, you learn about all kinds of furniture options. Have a seat."

He settled down next to her.

She pulled the table forward, caging them in. "Now reach down. At the bottom of the leg there's a little locking mechanism so our food won't roll away from us."

"Got it."

"Then let's eat." She spread her napkin in her lap. "Fabulous presentation."

"Thanks."

She picked up the pitcher and poured a generous amount of syrup over the crispy slices. As he waited for his turn with the syrup, he soaked up the ambiance. Firelight gleamed in her auburn curls and glowed in her dark eyes. He breathed in the combined aroma of wood smoke, cinnamon and Taryn's spicy scent. He wouldn't trade places with anyone in the world right now.

He quickly poured his syrup because evidently she was waiting for him before she began eating. He put down the pitcher. "Dig in."

"You don't have to tell me twice." Cutting off a thick piece with the side of her fork, she swirled it in a puddle of syrup, lifted the fork to her mouth and took her first bite.

It was rude to stare so he didn't, but her soft moan of pleasure was the sweetest sound he'd heard in ages. It also went straight to his groin. "Like it?"

"Mm-hm." She finished chewing and swallowed. "You can make this for me any old time you feel like it."

"Glad it hits the spot." He had permission to make French toast for her on a regular basis. Although it wasn't the activity he had in mind at this very moment, it was a start.

<u>10</u>

Well, wasn't this a recipe for disaster. Taryn ate the most amazing French toast of her life seated next to the virile cowboy who'd made it. A sexual buzz laced with a sugar high put her in a very precarious position.

Pete tempted her on an elemental level that her logical mind resisted and her body craved. A man who could make French toast this amazing had to be a very sensual person.

The evidence was clear tonight, but the signs had been there all along—the way he stroked Honey Butter's golden coat, the pleasure he took in spreading fresh-smelling straw in each stall, his comment about the softness of the blanket they'd put on the bed yesterday...

The bed incident should have clued her in, but it had taken this melt-in-your-mouth taste extravaganza to deliver the message in flashing neon. Chances were excellent that his sensuality would carry over into lovemaking. He would leave no inch of her body unexplored in a celebration of touch, taste and visual delight. He would breathe her in and relish her cries.

The longer she sat inches away from him the more she wanted him to do all of that. ASAP. Time to come up with a topic of conversation that wouldn't make her current agitation any worse. "Did you check the weather report for tomorrow?"

"No, can't say I did. And I left my phone in the kitchen."

"I'll get mine." She nudged the table aside just enough to escape the confining space. That was part of the problem, being so close to his stimulating self. She headed down the hall toward her bedroom where she'd left her phone.

As she picked it up, she glanced at her king-sized bed. Now there was a telling purchase. Although she wasn't looking for a sexual partner, she'd bought a king instead of a double or queen. Clearly she'd expected to share it with someone eventually. Just not the man currently ensconced on her sofa.

She carried her phone back to the living room and remained standing while she opened the weather app. "Tomorrow's predicted to be about the same as today. No precipitation, very little wind. Should be fine for what we want to do."

"Good to know."

Setting her phone on the coffee table, she glanced at the fireplace. Another welcome distraction. "The fire needs—"

"Let me." He carefully moved the table and stood. "I'm finished."

"All right. Thanks." She sat down and he moved the table back into place. With him available to lift furniture, wheels were superfluous.

"Do you want me to put on another log?"

"Better not. After I finish this I'll be ready for bed." Whoops.

"Me, too."

She paused, the fork halfway to her mouth.

"But I'll help you clean up before I go." He moved the screen and picked up the tongs.

"You cooked. I'll clean up." She went back to eating.

"Not the way I operate." After rearranging the chunks of blackened wood and coaxing the fire to life, he replaced the screen and turned back with a smile. "Unless you're trying to get rid of me."

She choked on her last bite of French toast.

"Uh-oh." He hurried over, moved the table and sat down. Then he rubbed her back. "You okay?"

She nodded, grabbed her napkin and coughed violently until the bit of food was dislodged and she could breathe normally again.

"Guess I hit a nerve." He continued to stroke her back. "Were you trying to get rid of me?"

She crumpled her napkin into a ball in her lap and cleared her throat. "In a way." She glanced at him. "But not because I don't want you here."

The mild concern in his eyes was replaced by simmering heat. "Then you *do* want me here?"

She didn't answer.

His gaze searched hers. "I'll go." He leaned forward and touched his mouth to hers in a slow, gentle kiss.

She closed her eyes, savoring the restrained passion in the light press of his lips. He knew. And he wouldn't take advantage of knowing.

He drew back. "Goodnight, Taryn."

She opened her eyes. He wouldn't take advantage, but his tender expression made it clear—one word from her and he'd stay. She swallowed. "Goodnight, Pete."

He smiled and inclined his head in silent acknowledgment. Then he stood, fetched his coat and hat from the hooks by the door, and let himself out.

* * *

Taryn slept well, and oh, the dreams. She longed to snuggle in her warm bed and replay them. Dreams were harmless, right? But she'd set her alarm so that she'd have plenty of time to feed the horses and turn them out before Pete arrived with the bucket truck.

After a quick breakfast eaten in the living room and illuminated by the glow of the Christmas tree, she bundled up. That first step into a Montana December morning was always the toughest. Stepping out on the porch, she put her hand on the master switch Pete had installed yesterday. "Let there be light!"

She flipped the switch. Twinkling lights on the porch and in the yard banished the darkness and flooded her with happiness. Hugging herself against the cold, she admired the display. She and Pete had done a terrific job and the pictures for her website would be beautiful.

Pete. What was she going to do about him? No point in pretending that she didn't want him even if she shouldn't want him. Clearly he'd be all in if she decided to go for it.

Then again, he was a guy. In her experience, they followed their animal instincts, aka the demands of Mr. Happy, and worried about the fallout later. She couldn't afford to do that.

In the days of knights in shining armor, they pledged their devotion to a woman but were content with a chaste relationship. At least that's what she'd been told. The reality might have been different. Knights might have climbed onto balconies and spent hours in their lady's bed.

Hours. Pete was strong and healthy. He'd have stamina. She gulped. Time to feed those critters.

Once she was inside the barn, she activated the lights along the roofline and the lighted wreath hung over the double door. Then she turned on another switch and the stalls were bathed in a warm glow.

The horses snorted and stomped as they roused themselves from sleep. She was here earlier than they were used to. "Rise and shine, gentlemen! It's a big day for Crimson Clouds Guest Ranch. You might even get your picture taken!"

Heads poked over stall doors—one a deep butterscotch with white mane and blaze, one a dappled gray with a dark gray mane that was a thing of beauty, and four who were just…brown. She'd learned to differentiate them after a week or so. She loved these six animals more than the ranch itself, and that was saying a lot.

Pulling on her work gloves, she filled the wheel barrow with hay flakes from the supply in a vacant stall. Then she started down the barn aisle delivering food, passing out loving words and bestowing friendly pats to Honey Butter, Fifty Shades, Marley, Buster, Spike and Junior.

They responded with nickers of welcome and soft head butts. They loved her, too. When she was in the barn with this crew, she basked in their good will. The sheer bulk of them was solid and comforting. Riding them had become a treat now that she'd developed some skill.

Her parents had favored small cuddly dogs as suitable family pets for their urban lifestyle and frequent travel plans. She'd enjoyed the heck out of those fluff balls, but given a choice, she'd take a horse.

As each one finished his breakfast, she led him out of the barn and turned him loose in the pasture. The sky had brightened to the color of vintage pearls by the time she took out the last horse. She had stalls to muck out, but she paused to lean against the fence as they cavorted in the pale light.

Not much could match the beauty of a horse in motion, muscles undulating, mane and tail rippling in the breeze.

The rumble of a truck's motor shifted her heart into high gear. Pete. She turned as he parked the truck, climbed out and walked toward her. Okay, that man rivaled the beauty of the horses.

His smile lit up the morning and his purposeful stride made her tingle with awareness. The time apart hadn't lessened his impact on her. If anything, it was stronger.

She gave him a nonchalant *hi, there.*

"Hi, yourself." His breath created puffs of fog in the cold air. "I see you turned on the lights."

"Couldn't resist."

"Are you sure you don't want them on a timer?"

"I'm sure. The ones on the trees, definitely on a timer. I won't be trudging out there to turn them off and on. But I like being able to decide when I want the others on. Like this morning. I didn't need them. I just wanted the effect."

"They were real pretty when I drove in. A festive way to start the day." He nudged back his hat. "Yours must have started earlier than mine."

"I thought we should get a jump on morning chores so we'd have maximum time with the bucket truck. All that's left is cleaning out the stalls." She kept her tone friendly but businesslike.

"Then let's get to it."

And that was that. No reason to reference last night's kiss or acknowledge a change in the status quo. Just move on. She headed for the barn. "Marley's not favoring his right front foot anymore."

He fell into step beside her. "That's good news. Did everybody else check out?"

"Yep. They're all looking healthy and happy."

"That's what we want."

Once they were in the barn, they slid right into their established routine, stripping off their coats and each grabbing gloves, a wheelbarrow and a rake. Pete always started with the last occupied stall and worked toward the front.

She began at the front with the optimistic goal of meeting him in the middle. It hadn't happened yet. He always cleaned four stalls to her two.

Not today. She was mucking out her third stall by the time he showed up ready to do it.

He chuckled. "Brought your A game, I see."

She glanced over her shoulder and grinned at him. "Or maybe you're slowing down."

His eyebrows lifted. "Maybe I no longer have something to prove."

"Are you implying that I do?"

"If the boot fits…"

She shrugged. "It's not a competition. My ego's not tied up in finishing this stall."

"You sure about that?"

"Absolutely." She walked into the aisle. "Be my guest. Rake away."

"Thanks. My ego's totally tied up in this." He flashed her a smile and got to work.

<u>11</u>

Joking around was one of Pete's favorite methods for releasing tension. Physical work was another, which was why he was delighted to finish Taryn's job on that last stall. He could have done ten more.

Funny thing was, she'd guessed right. He'd slowed down this morning. More than once he'd caught himself staring into space, Taryn on his mind. He wasn't sure what to do about it.

Stringing those tree lights was next on the agenda and he'd invited her to take a ride with him in the bucket. He'd reserved a double bucket so he could follow through on that invite. Close quarters, nevertheless, and last night's kiss was driving him nucking futs.

After they'd gathered all the packages of large white lights and loaded them in a storage compartment in the back of the truck, he helped her into the passenger side of the cab and off they went. She was super excited. Although she wasn't literally bouncing on the seat, she looked as if she'd like to.

He drove slowly over the frozen ground to the grove of trees. "I didn't ask if you want to go for a short ride and be done, or if you want to stay up there with me and help me string lights."

"Could I help?"

"If you have the time. I wasn't clear on how much more you need to accomplish before Caitlin gets here."

"Mostly some inside decorations. I was also thinking of making evergreen swags to hang on each of the stall doors so she could shoot inside the barn, too."

"That's a great idea. So maybe you only want a short ride in the bucket so you can go back and work on those things."

"Actually, I'd love to stay up there and help you string the lights. It sounds like fun."

"It is fun. Glad to have you." He might as well get used to this persistent ache when she was around. Evidently she didn't want to take the relationship further and he was here for the duration. Stalemate.

"I supervised holiday decorations at the hotel I managed, but I didn't dive in and help make it happen, either putting up or taking down. We didn't talk about when we'd do the second part."

"I made a command decision and reserved the truck for January seventh. That's when Dad and I took ours down at the Lazy S, weather permitting, but I can change it if—"

"That's good. The day after Epiphany. That's when my folks took stuff down, too."

"I also wondered if you'd like me to go ahead and reserve the truck for next year. I could handle that when I take it back today."

"Absolutely. I want to make this a tradition, except we can start earlier, like maybe the end of November."

"And add more lights?"

She laughed. "You know me too well."

Not nearly well enough. "Then I'll make a reservation for next year." He parked parallel to the trees. "You wanted the lights on these three, right?"

"Yep. It'll look better lighting three together instead of doing alternate ones."

"Got it. Ready to do this thing?"

"I'm so ready."

He grabbed his hard hat from the dash and handed the other one to her. "Better get this on." He exited the truck and went around to help her down. Maybe this wasn't such a bad idea, after all. She would love it.

And there was something about a pretty woman in a hard hat. "That's a good look on you. Very badass."

"I know!" She zipped up her parka. "I feel like I should be singing *Wichita Lineman*."

"Trust me, you'll never be mistaken for a lineman."

"Thanks for that. I'm loving the hard hat, though. I think I was a construction worker in another life." She gazed at him. "Do I have it on backwards?"

"No. Why?"

"You're staring at me and grinning. I thought I might have it on wrong."

"It's on right. It's also very cute. Makes me smile." He pulled on his gloves. "Let me grab the blocks for the wheels." Once he'd made sure the truck was stable, he helped her climb onto the truck bed and into the bucket. Then he opened the storage compartment and started handing her boxes of lights. "Just stack them in the middle."

"Okay."

His considerable experience stringing holiday lights at the Lazy S with his dad was coming in handy. Creating that display had been one of his favorite jobs and he was glad Taryn had decided to do this. If his chest was a little tight at the prospect of spending time with her in the cozy bucket, oh, well. He'd live.

"Last one." He handed her the final box of lights and joined her in the bucket. "We'll start from the bottom. And here we go." The morning was quiet except for the soft purr of the crane's motor as he maneuvered the bucket away from the truck and toward the first tree.

"This is *awesome*." Taryn gripped the side of the bucket, her expression animated. "Almost makes me want to switch occupations and become a lineman, after all."

"It's all fun and games until you're handling high-voltage wires."

"Yeah, there's that. Maybe I'll just stick with helping you string lights in pine trees." She opened the first box and took out the strand of lights. "Let me know when you're ready."

"Almost." He positioned the bucket next to the covered outlet he'd attached high on the trunk yesterday, along with a timer that he'd already programmed. "Okay. First strand, starting with the male plug."

"I figured as much." She handed over the end of the cord and fed him the strand slowly as he maneuvered the bucket. "I always wondered how it came to be called that."

He plugged the lights into the timer and began looping the cord over the branches. "I'd say it's obvious."

"Of course it is, but is it necessary? We don't call a bolt male and a nut female."

"Actually, sometimes construction folks do designate them that way. Same with pipe fittings." He raised the bucket and started back across the front branches of the tree.

"Again, why is it necessary? Why not just use Part A and Part B instead of using sexual references?"

"Not as descriptive. Using A and B won't tell the same story. Whereas this labeling method tells you exactly, I'd even say elegantly, what to expect. If you insert male prongs into a female receptacle, electricity flows." And in his determination to make his point, he'd turned himself on. *Nice going, Sawyer.*

"Guess so." She took a deep breath.

And he'd turned her on, too, judging by all the air she'd sucked in just now. "Didn't mean to get so explicit."

"I'm the one who asked."

"You happened to hit on a subject dear to my heart. I love the designation. I wish everything in life could be as straightforward and easy to understand as electrical plugs." He took the controls and raised the bucket a little more. "We must be about to the end of this strand."

"We are. Just hang out for a minute while I open another box."

"Glad to. It's nice up here." The shrill cry of a red-tailed hawk caught his attention. It circled overhead and was soon joined by another, slightly smaller one.

"The next strand's ready to go."

"Thanks." He moved the bucket and kept going. "I'll bet that's a mated pair of hawks circling above us. I saw them yesterday when I was working out here."

"Are we disturbing them?"

"If we are, it's just temporary. Assuming they've been living this close to the house and the barn all along, they can't be too upset seeing us out here. Anyway, we'll be gone soon and they'll have their favorite perches back."

"Okay, good. I don't want to screw up life for a pair of hawks because I want some Christmas lights in the pine trees."

"I doubt you will. My dad's a nut about taking the wildlife into account and we had way more lights up than this."

"More than at Wild Creek?'

He laughed. "No. That display is epic. At least to me. I'm a country boy. San Francisco likely goes all out for the holiday."

"It does. That might be why I'm so light-crazy."

"So what are your favorite displays there?"

"I don't know if I can choose."

"Then tell me about all of them."

"It's a long list, but here goes." She glowed with enthusiasm as she described the decorations in Union Square, Ghirardelli Square and Fisherman's Wharf. He kept asking questions, prompting her to continue.

"Are you sure I'm not boring you?"

"Not at all. I've never been there. You're giving me a great picture of the place." The topic was interesting enough, but that special lilt in her voice was what he was after. He could listen to it all day. And all night, for that matter.

"Okay, then." She told him about the huge light display at the Embarcadero, the ice skating rink, the tree lighting ceremony at Golden Gate Park and the two-story gingerbread house in the Fairmont Hotel. "I think that's enough," she said at last. "Besides, this is the last strand of lights."

"Yep, we're almost done. But I'm curious, since you clearly love your hometown, why didn't you go back for Christmas, even if your folks weren't going to be there?"

"I had friends who wanted me to come and stay with them. But just like I didn't want to spend time in London when I could be here getting ready for my guests, I didn't want to be in San Francisco, either. This ranch is the most important thing in my life right now."

And he was part of that. Good enough. He looped the end of the strand around a branch so it would stay put. "Then I guess it's important that you came up here with me, so you can get a really great view of it." He raised the bucket to its maximum height and swiveled it so she was facing away from the trees. "Take a look. There's your ranch."

She gave a little gasp of delight. "It's *beautiful* from up here. Can you see how gracefully the buildings are nestled in the trees?"

"Yep. You get a real appreciation of that from here."

"Even better, the cabins I added flow with the rest of the buildings. They look as if they've been there all along. I planned it that way, but now that I see it laid out from this vantage point...it really works."

"It does. You've done a great job."

"You know how I'd like to commemorate this moment up here with you?"

A kiss? Did he dare hope? "How?"

"Take a selfie of the two of us."

He quickly downgraded his expectations. "Sure, why not?"

"Could you please take it?" She held out her phone. "You have longer arms."

"I'll do my best. I'm no expert at this, though. I've done it maybe twice." He pulled off his gloves, shoved them in his pocket and took her phone. "You'll have to coach me."

"First we need to get closer." She moved in next to him, nudging the empty light boxes out of the way. Then she wrapped her arm around his waist and snuggled in.

He could do no less than put his arm around her waist and nestle her against him. Selfies rocked. "Now what?"

"Click that little symbol in the bottom right corner so the camera focuses on us."

He managed that, and there they were in the frame, Taryn smiling and looking adorable in her hard hat, him looking...dazed and confused, but happy.

"Bring your head down next to mine so our cheeks are almost touching. That's better."

Certainly was.

"Now put your thumb on the shutter in the middle and smile." She kept her smile in place while she said that, which had to be a learned skill. He couldn't talk and smile at the same time.

A happy face was easy, though, when her warm body was tucked in close and her spicy scent tickled his nose. He tapped the button with his thumb.

"I don't think that took. I didn't hear the squeal-click."

"Squeal-click?" He looked at her. "What's that?"

She turned her head, which brought her very, very close. She swallowed and her eyelashes fluttered. "The noise it makes when...it takes a picture." Her gaze dropped to his mouth.

"Oh."

Her voice grew breathy. "You must not...take many pictures."

"I don't." His heart thudded with almost painful intensity.

Then she slowly closed her eyes.

Yes. He had to tilt his head to avoid a hard-hat collision, but he was motivated. Once he had the angle right, the space between his lips and hers disappeared as if by magic. He touched down and she whimpered. He increased the pressure and she moaned.

Or maybe that was him. He lost track. Her lips parted, inviting him in, blocking out everything but the heat, the fire, and a high-pitched whirring noise....

12

So perfect. So right. Taryn surrendered without firing a shot. *This.* Oh, yes, *this.* Pete's supple mouth, the arousing thrust of his tongue, the anticipation of—what the heck was that noise?

Oh. She drew back, gasping for breath. "Pete."

His eyes fluttered open to reveal a gaze dark with passion. "What?"

"You're...taking...pictures."

He blinked, looked over at the phone, and lifted his thumb. The noise stopped.

She stared at him as hot desire slowly morphed into the urge to giggle.

He stared back. Then his eyes began to twinkle. "How many do you suppose I took?"

She grinned. "Hundreds."

"*Hundreds*?"

"If you hold the shutter down it takes ten pictures per second."

He laughed and shook his head. "Hundreds."

"Uh-huh."

"Of us kissing."

"Yep."

"I want to see one." He tapped the phone. "Only eight hundred and twenty-seven? We kissed longer than that."

"It seems longer when you're out in the forest."

He smiled. "You're a funny lady." His gaze held hers and gradually his smile faded. "No matter how long it was, I loved every second."

"So did I." Couldn't very well deny it. He'd been there. He knew.

"I'd like to try it again sometime when we're on solid—oops, someone's calling you." He checked the screen before handing it over. "Caitlin."

She took the phone and put it on speaker. "Hi, Caitlin."

"Hey, Taryn. Listen I know you aren't expecting me until later, but my midday appointment cancelled. I'd like to come over and spend time getting acclimated, maybe set up some indoor shots while I wait for the lights to come on. Would that be okay?"

"That would be fine. We just finished lighting some of the bigger trees. We're planning to do some decorating in the barn, but—"

"Here's an idea. Let me take some video of you decorating the barn. People love seeing a work in progress."

"Um, okay. Just me?"

"How about you and that good-looking foreman of yours?"

Pete rolled his eyes.

"I'll check and see if he's up for being in the video."

"Excellent. I can be out there in about twenty minutes or less."

"See you then." Taryn disconnected the call and glanced at him. "You okay with being in the video I put on my website?"

"Might as well add to my film credits."

"Oh?"

"My dad and Kendra already previewed Monday night's video, and there are several seconds of me helping Josh play the kazoo."

"I'm not surprised. That was a very video-worthy moment."

"I guess. Anyway, we'd better get a move on if she'll be here in less than twenty minutes."

"Yep. I'd like to tidy up the living room and maybe you could cut some pine branches for the barn decorations."

"Will do." He gazed at her. "Please don't delete those pictures, okay?"

"I can't keep eight hundred and twenty-seven of them."

"I know. But I'd like a chance to scroll through them when there's time."

"Um, okay." She'd allowed herself to be caught up in the moment. Now she had to figure out what the heck to do about it. She'd kissed him. With gusto.

"Best bucket truck experience ever."

"It's my only one so it has to be my best ever." One steamy kiss. She could still dial it back, right?

"Take my word for it. Doesn't get any better than this." He turned away and reached for the controls. The bucket slowly descended.

Time to change the subject. "I wonder if Caitlin will want the horses to be in their stalls."

"She might. More interesting that way. Should I round 'em up and bring 'em in?"

"No, let's wait until she gets here. She might want to shoot you rounding them up."

"I doubt it. Nothing special about herding horses from the pasture to the barn."

She smiled. He had no idea that he created a stirring visual when he was out there working with those magnificent animals. "It might be special to a person sitting in a busy office and dreaming of a guest ranch vacation."

"That's a good point. I have a tough time imagining what that would be like. I wouldn't last a day."

Which was a huge part of his appeal. A man who'd chosen a rugged outdoor life and demanded a certain amount of personal freedom was sexy. A video of Pete wrangling beautiful horses would help sell this place, especially to women. Until Caitlin's casual remark about her *good-looking foreman* she hadn't thought of that.

When Pete maneuvered the bucket back into the bed of the truck, the ride ended, almost as if they'd arrived at the station after a journey. Not a bad analogy, either. Now that he was helping her out of the bucket and back into the cab, their passionate kiss while suspended forty feet above the ground didn't seem quite real.

She'd come down to earth. Her stomach rumbled, reminding her that breakfast had been hours ago. "Even though Caitlin's due any minute, we still need to eat lunch. I'll make sandwiches and coffee. Just come up to the house after you cut a few branches and we'll grab a bite."

"I will."

She took off her hard hat and laid it on the dash next to his as he pulled up in front of the house and put the truck in neutral. "Just let me hop—" But she was wasting her breath. He was already out the door and coming around.

He opened her door and held out his hand.

"Honestly, Pete, you don't have to do this every time." But she put her hand in his because he was right there, smiling at her.

"What if I like doing it?" He steadied her on the way down.

"That's what you always say, but—"

"I do like it." He closed the passenger door. "It's my way of being respectful. See you soon." Walking quickly around to the driver's door, he climbed in and drove toward the barn.

The low growl of a vehicle navigating her dirt road announced Caitlin's arrival. A classic Jeep Cherokee, its white sides mud-spattered, approached.

Caitlin pulled in, shut off the engine and climbed out. Her purple knit hat was the same one she'd had on Monday night, but instead of leaving her brown hair loose, she'd plaited it into two braids that hung past her shoulders. "How'd the tree-trimming go?"

"Like clockwork." Except for a kiss that nearly made her phone explode.

"I'll leave my Jeep here while I unpack my gear, then move it out of the way."

"Need any help carrying?"

"That'd be great." Her running shoes crunching on the gravel as she started toward the back of the Jeep. "If business keeps up like this, I'll be able to hire an assistant, but for now, it's just me." She glanced at the decorated arch and wagon wheels. "Nice job. Bet it's pretty when the lights come on."

"I'm insanely proud of it. Especially considering Pete and I had so little time to pull it together."

"Pete's your foreman?"

"Right."

"Has he agreed to be in the video?"

"Yep."

"Good. He's a photogenic dude. I got a tight shot of him Monday night and I'm hoping he'll give me permission to use the clip on my website." She opened the back of the Jeep.

"Can't wait to see it."

"I brought my laptop. I can show it to both of you while I'm here. If you could grab the laptop and my tripod, I can get the rest."

"Be glad to." Taryn helped carry her gear into the house. "I was about to fix some lunch and make coffee." She unzipped her parka. "Can I get you anything?"

"I've had lunch, but coffee would be awesome." She slid her large backpack off her shoulders and set it by the door. "Beautiful living room." After shoving the purple hat in the pocket of her jacket, she took it off and hung it next to Taryn's on one of the hooks by the door. "Would you be willing to make a fire to add ambiance?"

"I'd planned on it."

"Then we're on the same page—fireplace blazing, tree lit, comfy furniture to cradle the weary bones of stressed-out city dwellers."

"Exactly! I knew you were the right person for this job."

Caitlin smiled. "I did, too." She crouched next to her backpack. "Is it okay if I turn on some lights? I'd like to take some preliminary stills."

"Have at it. I'll be in the kitchen if you need me." She went in, started the coffee and quickly pulled out sandwich fixings.

Ten minutes later, she came out of the kitchen with a sandwich and a mound of chips on each plate just as Pete walked through the door.

He greeted Caitlin before turning to her with a grin. "How's that for timing?"

"Impressive." She set the plates on the game table. "Caitlin has Monday night's video on her laptop. I vote we all get our coffee and watch the video while you and I eat."

"Works for me." He took off his jacket and hat. "I just need to wash up."

Moments later they gathered at the table and Caitlin accessed the video on her laptop. "There's a section of this where you're prominently featured, Pete. You and little Josh."

"So I've heard."

"It's cute as hell. Makes me laugh every time. If you're willing to sign a release, I'd like to use it on my website to promote my work."

"Um, yeah, sure. If it's okay with Gage and Emma."

"They're fine with it."

"Then so am I."

Taryn picked up her sandwich, intending to eat it as she watched. Then she put it down again, unwilling to chance missing something.

Caitlin had done a fabulous job of capturing the spirit of the event. She'd added hushed Christmas instrumentals to the opening scenes as the crowd arrived and climbed the hill to the A-frame. The element of secrecy and excitement built to a crescendo as Deidre mounted the ladder and the caroling began.

Close-ups of everyone on the balcony were blended with wide shots of Eagles Nesters belting out those songs with gusto. Then the mood changed as the tender melody of *Silent Night* filled the clearing. And there was Pete, making sure that Josh could participate.

The little boy was so into it. He blew spit everywhere and waved his arms, smacking his obliging uncle several times in the face. Taryn laughed right along with Pete and Caitlin.

The video ended, as it should, with more close-ups of Faith, Cody, Kendra, the baby in Kendra's arms, and the proud grandfathers, Quinn and Jim. Those folks were the stars of the show.

That said, Pete and Josh's segment was her absolute favorite. Josh was cute, no question. But the image of Pete, his expression alight with love, was unforgettable.

Caitlin was right. The guy was photogenic. And she had eight hundred and twenty-seven pictures of him on her phone.

13

Sure enough, Caitlin wanted footage of him wrangling those horses. Pete couldn't see the advantage of a video like that, but Taryn was on board with the idea, too. She wanted it to be all him, too. She wouldn't be part of it.

After lunch they headed outside. Caitlin glanced over at him as they neared the barn. "How do you usually do this?"

He shrugged. "Nothing much to it. We get lead ropes from the barn, attach 'em to a couple of horses, take those in, go back for two more, and so on. Like I said, not very exciting."

"What if you rode one of the horses bareback and used him to round up the others?"

"Not really necessary. They like us. They usually come right over. If you'll excuse me a minute, I'll go get those ropes." When he returned, the two women were talking up a storm.

Taryn faced him. "We've scripted a more dramatic scenario, something that will be fun to watch."

He nudged back his hat. "Don't know how you can make a simple chore dramatic."

"It would be if you rounded them up like Caitlin suggested. You could start by walking out there, grabbing a handful of Honey Butter's mane and vaulting onto his back."

"But there's no reason to—"

"It'll look amazing, Pete," Caitlin said. "People who've never been on a ranch will love a video of that. Oh, and Taryn mentioned seeing you do it, so I know it's in your repertoire."

"I was just goofing around." Showboating for Taryn. Served him right that she'd want him to repeat that stunt for the cameras. If anyone in his family saw this video they'd laugh themselves silly. He'd never hear the end of it.

"Then please go goof around." Taryn's gaze sparkled with excitement. "Ham it up. If it convinces a whole lot of people to make reservations, that'll be great for both of us."

"Yes, ma'am." Like he could refuse her anything, especially when she looked at him like that. She also might have a point. He'd never worked on a guest ranch before.

At the Lazy S, he and his dad had sold healthy, well-trained horses, not a fantasy of Western life. Yet that was exactly what Taryn was selling. The bed they'd put together on Monday was proof of that.

He handed her the lead ropes. "What's supposed to happen once I get them organized?"

"I'll stop filming," Caitlin said. "Because you're right. Clipping lead ropes on them and leading them into the barn isn't particularly exciting. If you could take your time rounding them up, maybe make it look harder than it is, that would be wonderful."

"So essentially I'm putting on an act."

"To some extent." Taryn looped the ropes over her arm. "A big part of hospitality is presenting good theater. You're entertaining people who come expecting a certain experience. If you give them that experience, they're happy. They come back, they spread the word to others, and the location thrives."

"Alrighty, then." He touched two fingers to the brim of his hat. "Ladies." And he sauntered off toward the pasture, grinning. Oh, yeah, he'd get ragged unmercifully by his loving family if they saw this clip, but if he had to do it, he might as well have fun. One Hollywood cowboy, coming up.

Honey Butter was grazing peacefully about ten yards away. Pete called out to the palomino, who lifted his head and continued chewing.

"Wanna be a movie star, Honey Butter? We'll be a team, you and me. I'll be the stunt man and you'll be the trick horse. Got it?"

The gelding just looked at him, eyelids at half-mast. Unimpressed.

"You can't just stand there while I climb aboard. Get a move on, son." He slapped the horse's hindquarters. Honey Butter snorted and trotted off.

"Much better." Pete loped after him, grabbed a hunk of mane while they were both in motion, and vaulted smoothly onto his back. He used to have fun doing that when he was a teenager. Still did.

Then he leaned over the horse's silky neck. "Pedal to the metal time, Honey Butter." Tightening his leg muscles, he applied pressure to the gelding's ribs. "*Ha!*" And they were off, galloping around the pasture.

Naturally that stirred up the other five, who decided it must be frolic time. Herding the gallivanting horses into a cohesive group was tricky, but not as difficult as he made it look.

He drew the process out until they were clearly getting sick of the game. Then he drove them toward the gate. "How was that?"

"Great!" Caitlin lowered her camera. "Exactly what I was looking for."

"I just had a thought." He slid down and looked at Taryn. "Won't some of the guests who've seen that video expect the same kind of nonsen—uh, I mean *performance* when they get here?"

"They might." She opened the gate and came in with two of the lead ropes. "Would you have a problem doing it every so often?"

"I suppose not. The horses seemed to get a charge out of it." He clipped a lead rope to Honey Butter's halter. "Bet you'd like to escort this bad boy in."

"Sure would." She took the rope and stroked the gelding's white blaze. "Hey, buddy. You looked terrific out there, mane and tail flying, coat flashing in the sun."

"Speaking of the sun…" Pete glanced up at the sky. "We're burning daylight and I have to have the truck back by four."

"Then let's get these boys in their stalls and start decorating." She glanced at him. "Thanks for cooperating. I hope it didn't pain you too much to do it."

"To be honest, it was kind of fun." Getting a chance to show off for her wasn't all bad.

After the horses were tucked into their stalls, he brought in the pile of evergreen branches he'd cut and Taryn went back to the house for red ribbon and wire. While Caitlin filmed them, they made swags for the stall doors and hung them low enough that the horses wouldn't be able to lean over and start nibbling.

Caitlin couldn't talk because her comments would be picked up on the video. She'd encouraged them to make conversation, though, so they wouldn't come off as robotic.

They'd agreed on a topic prior to the start of shooting—favorite holiday traditions. They'd compared experiences with stockings, treats for Santa, and opening presents.

He saved his best one until they were almost finished. He wired the last swag and passed it to her so she could add the ribbon. "In my family, we always go down to the barn about ten minutes before midnight."

"What for?" She concentrated on the bow she was creating.

"Legend says that at midnight the horses are given the gift of speech."

She glanced up in surprise. "And do they talk?"

He loved that instead of laughing at the idea, she was willing to believe it might be possible. "I can't say. I've never heard them, but that doesn't mean it's not true."

"And you go every Christmas Eve?"

"Got to. It's tradition. Maybe this will be the year I'll hear them say something."

"Like what?"

"I've thought about that. Ever since I got Clifford when I was sixteen, I've expected him to say *change my name, damn it.* He never has, so he continues to be Clifford, which is the name he had when he arrived at the Lazy S."

"I'm assuming we'll still be at Wild Creek at midnight. Do you know if Kendra has that tradition?"

"Don't know, but now that my dad's in the picture, I'll bet it'll become part of the mix. I've never known him to miss that barn visit on Christmas Eve."

"I want to do it, too. Although now that I think about it, I'd rather be in this barn, with these guys. I'd love to hear what they have to say."

"Then we'll come back here before midnight."

"But that means leaving your family."

He smiled. "I'll have spent hours with them by then, and considering how many people will be in that ranch house on Christmas Eve, they'll have a crowd going down to the barn. I'd rather be here with you."

Damn. That revealing statement was now recorded for posterity. He'd completely lost track of Caitlin and her camcorder.

Evidently he'd gone all deer-in-the-headlights, because Taryn dropped her gaze to the ribbon she was arranging and lowered her voice. "No worries. She'll edit that out."

He nodded, but wasn't willing to take it as a given. Before he left to return the bucket truck he found a moment to talk privately with Caitlin.

"I'd already planned to take it out." Her gaze was kind. "The video is designed to promote the ranch, not reveal a budding romance between you two."

"We're just good friends."

Caitlin smiled. "Good friends make great lovers."

That caught him flat-footed. He couldn't come up with anything but a quick *yes, ma'am*. Then he said goodbye to Taryn and left before he managed to snarl himself up even worse.

He'd been prepared to return the bucket truck and come back to feed, but Taryn had insisted it wasn't necessary. The horses were already in their stalls, so all she had left was delivering hay flakes. Which was true, but she also might be playing it safe.

He got it. Despite her passionate response during the selfie incident, she was still debating the pros and cons. He could see it in her eyes whenever he caught her looking at him.

The lights hadn't come on in the trees by the time he pulled away from the ranch, but tomorrow was good enough. He'd see them first thing in the morning when he drove in. He could wait.

After returning the truck and booking next year's reservation, he hopped in his pickup and headed for home. A gray sedan he didn't recognize was parked in front of the house. Looked like an airport rental.

Parking his truck, he hurried up to the house, eager to find out if his guess about the car and its driver was correct. By the time his boots hit the porch steps, he had the answer. The laughter coming from inside the house clinched it. Uncle Brendan had arrived.

He walked through the door and his uncle was already on his feet, coming toward him. "Damn it, Pete, you're bigger and better lookin' than I remember." He gave him a fierce hug. "Come on back to 'stralia with me, mate. My boss could use that kind of muscle and I know several ladies who'd be delighted to meet you."

"Sorry. Not interested." He loved hearing the accent his uncle had picked up from thirty years of working Down Under. Very Crocodile Dundee. "I like it fine right where I am." He accepted the beer his dad handed him. "Thanks, Dad."

"Have a seat, son. Kendra will be over shortly and I've notified everyone else that this crazy guy's finally turned up. Plane was early. Good thing I was home."

"Yea, yea, no worries if you hadn't been, big brother. I'd have let myself in and helped myself to your beer." *Beer* came out as *beah.* He reclaimed his spot on the couch and picked up the bottle he'd left on an end table. "Not a bad brew, either." He examined the bottle. "I could grow to actually like it."

Pete took the other end of the couch. "When did you get in?"

"'bout an hour ago. Good thing you're sitting downwind. I could use a shower after more'n twenty-four hours in the air, but Quinn shoved a beer in my hand and I gave up the idea for the time being."

"You look pretty good, considering." Pete hadn't seen his uncle in a couple of years, but he hadn't changed much, still tanned and fit from wrangling horses at a dude ranch. His hair might be slightly grayer, but that was to be expected when he was nearing fifty.

He smiled. "Thanks. Nice little town you have, but it's a helluva lot harder to get to than Spokane. Easier to navigate the Outback."

Pete's dad settled back in his favorite easy chair. "Then save yourself the trouble and move here."

"You should," Pete said. "Add one more to the growing Sawyer population."

"And what's up with that? First I hear that Roxanne migrated down this way, and next thing I know, it's a stampede of Sawyers. It's nice that you're all bunched up so I can see the lot of you at one go, but damn, is the place really that spectacular?"

"It's a great town," his dad said. "But as I was telling you when Pete showed up, that wasn't my motivation."

"And speakin' of your motivation." He glanced at his watch, a classic he'd had ever since Pete could remember. "Isn't she overdue? I thought she said ten minutes or so."

"She did, but she could have been sidetracked by that grandbaby."

"Yeah, that's the other news I can't wrap my head around. My big brother's a grandpa and he's coupled up with a grandma. How does *that* feel?"

His dad smiled. "Terrific."

"Hard to imagine." He glanced at Pete. "You and me, mate. The only remainin' single Sawyers."

"Looks like it."

"So you haven't been bitten by the love bug that seems to be runnin' rampant in this town?"

"No, sir." *What about that kiss, hotshot?*

"So glad to hear it." His uncle raised his beer bottle. "To the Sawyer bachelors."

"Proud to be in the club, Uncle Brendan." Pete tapped his bottle against his uncle's and took a long swallow. He'd gone along with the toast because it seemed like the thing to do, but his heart wasn't in it.

"Quinn tells me you're followin' in my footsteps, working at a dude ranch."

"That I am."

"And your boss is a single lady?"

"Yep."

"Pretty?"

He hesitated. Saying the truth, that she was beautiful, would put too fine a point on his feelings about the matter.

"She's very attractive," his dad said. "Nice, too. I finally met her at Roxanne and Michael's wedding last month."

His uncle nodded. "Pretty and nice. That's a lethal combination, Pete. If you like the job, listen to your Uncle Brendan. Steer clear. That's a situation that can fall apart faster than a jackaroo can guzzle a pint."

Pete gazed at him. "Speaking from experience, are you?"

"I had a near miss. That's all I'm sayin'."

_14_

After Caitlin left, Taryn made a quick run to the Eagles Nest Market to stock up on enough groceries to get her through the next few days. Then she stopped by the Guzzling Grizzly Country Store and picked up two bottles of the wine Kendra liked. Back home again, she wasted no time putting everything away. She'd been waiting for a spare moment all day.

Grabbing her phone, she walked into the living room and opened her picture app. _Oh._ One glance at the image of _the kiss_ and she was standing in the bucket, knees weak and heart pounding. Moisture pooled in her mouth.

She scrolled to the next picture, which wasn't any different. She swiped faster, turning the shots into a mini-movie. Sinking down to the couch, she swallowed and kept going. Her lips tingled and her chest grew tight. And hot. She was so hot.

There. She paused the action. That was the moment he'd gone deeper, the moment she'd _invited_ him to go deeper. She kept scrolling, gripping the phone and squirming against the cushion. Then it was over. Last picture. She gulped for air and pressed the phone to her galloping heart.

This was crazy. It was a kiss, for God's sake. One very short kiss. Putting down the phone, she left the couch and snatched her parka off the hook by the door.

The Christmas lights were still on. Zipping her parka as she crossed the porch, she pulled up her hood and shoved her hands in her pockets. Cold air was her friend. She hurried past the glittering spruce trees and under the lighted arch.

Movement was good, too. She race-walked across the open area between the house and the barn and finally stopped when her chest ached. Dragging icy air into her lungs, she gazed at the lighted trees in the grove.

You had to look, didn't you?

Gradually her breathing slowed and her head cleared. One kiss. Well, two, if she counted the one from French toast night. But it wasn't like she'd slept with him. She could still turn things around, get back on solid, platonic ground.

Wouldn't be easy, though. Why did he have to be so sexy? And such a good guy? If she did sleep with him she could risk everything she was working toward.

So she wouldn't sleep with him. Decision made. She needed to delete those pictures, too. Unfortunately, she'd promised him she wouldn't, at least not until he'd seen them. She wasn't in the habit of breaking promises. In any case, she wouldn't look at them again.

* * *

Taryn was loading her breakfast dishes in the dishwasher when she heard Pete's truck. She finished, quickly grabbed her parka, and headed outside. Much colder than last night. Brrr.

The trees in the grove were on already, but she had to manually turn on the house and yard Christmas lights. They hadn't welcomed Pete this morning. Maybe a timer for the house and yard was a good idea, after all.

As she left the porch and headed for the barn, he parked beside it. Then he got out, walked over until he had a good view of the grove, and gazed at it, hands on his hips.

"Aren't the lights amazing?" She hurried toward him, holding the furry edges of her hood against her face with her gloved hands.

He turned to her and smiled. "Not bad. If I still had the bucket truck, I'd fix that one spot."

"Which spot?" She stood beside him and squinted at the lights while she tried not to shiver. "Looks fabulous to me."

"Pretty much, but there's one place on the last tree where I'm not happy with how I looped the strand. The light pattern's not as symmetrical."

"I c-can't see what you're t-talking about."

"Right there." He put his arm around her shoulders and turned her a little while he pointed toward a middle section of the tree. "Between the eighth and ninth rows of lights. Too much of a gap."

She wasn't cold anymore. "Okay. I see it, but I doubt anyone else would." He was so warm and cozy. If he kissed her right now, even her toes would be toasty. *No sleeping with Pete, no sleeping with Pete.*

He sucked in a breath, released her and stepped away. "Next year we should keep the truck overnight so we can fix anything that shows up after the fact." He tugged down the brim of his Stetson, making it tougher to read his expression.

"Good idea." Whatever impulse had prompted him to put his arm around her, he'd clearly thought better of it. Maybe he'd come to the same conclusion she had. "Also, I've decided a timer on the house and yard lights is a good idea, after all."

"I'll set it up today, then." He started toward the barn.

"Did you see the weather on TV last night?"

"I did. My uncle arrived yesterday. When he saw that report, he was glad he'd beat the snowstorm."

"So he did come after all! Can't wait to meet him."

"He's the same Uncle Brendan, living the life. Seems perfectly happy to be an Aussie jackaroo. Almost sounds like a native, calling people *mate* and dropping his r's."

"Does he wear an Aussie-style hat?"

"No, he still wears a Stetson." He slid back the bar holding the barn doors closed. "We all thought he'd get sick of living so far away, but he claims he'd miss the howl of the dingoes."

"Over here he could listen to wolves." She stepped inside the warm barn and ditched her parka.

"Wolves, coyotes, owls—you'd think he could make do with them, but evidently not. Watching that movie as a teenager changed his life."

"Is he younger or older than your dad?" She put hay flakes in her wheelbarrow and moved to the front of the barn.

"Younger, but not by much. Less than two years, I think." Pete loaded his wheelbarrow. "You can see that younger brother versus older brother thing going on. My dad's the steady, responsible one and my uncle's the guy who ran off to find adventure in Australia."

"Kind of like you and Gage."

"Kind of like that, only now Gage is a dedicated family man and I'm the one with no strings. As my uncle pointed out last night, we're the only two Sawyer bachelors left."

"He never got married?"

"He was engaged for a while, but when she balked at moving to Australia, they split."

"If he was that crazy about the place, seems like something they'd discuss before getting engaged." She delivered a hay flake to Honey Butter and paused to give the palomino a scratch. "But I'm not one to talk. I didn't look before I leaped, either."

"Not a long courtship?" His tone was casual, but he'd never asked about her ex before. That made the question anything but casual.

"Nope. We were engaged within six weeks of meeting each other and married two months later."

"How'd you meet him?"

"At a masked ball."

"No kidding? That sounds like something out of a movie."

"That was the idea behind the fundraiser. It's an extremely romantic idea to dress in elegant clothes and add a beautiful half-mask to hide your identity." She moved her wheelbarrow and grabbed another hay flake.

"I guess it would be. The only mask I ever wore was when I dressed up as Jason from *Friday the 13th*."

"Yeah, that's not romantic."

"When you're a ten-year-old boy you want to scare girls and make them scream."

"So did you?"

"Yeah, but it wasn't as fun as I thought it would be. I made one girl cry and I ended up taking off the mask and apologizing for scaring her."

She smiled. "Now *that's* romantic." She met him in the barn aisle as they each finished feeding. "Should we turn them out? It seems super cold this morning."

"That's because it is. But they can handle it much better than we can. I'll take them out if you—"

"Thanks for the offer, but I'm helping. I like doing it, even when it's cold. I sometimes forget that they're different from us, though. I make the mistake of thinking of them as big dogs. And a dog would want to stay where it's warm."

"Not these guys. Unless they have a problem, they'd much rather be outside." Pete took both their jackets down and handed over her parka. "On the other hand, I don't intend to lollygag while we're taking them out there."

She laughed. "Yeah, me, either."

It might've been the fastest turnout they'd ever done. Taryn always enjoyed the satisfaction of mucking out the stalls, but this morning it was also a great way to warm up again.

Pete was on his game today. He was finishing up his fourth stall while she put the final touches on her second. That gave him time to dump the wheelbarrows in the compost pile while she used a pitchfork to spread out a thick bed of straw.

She glanced up when he came back inside. "Hey, speed demon. Who put a quarter in you this morning?"

He leaned against the open stall door. "I stayed up late listening to Uncle Brendan's stories. Moving fast keeps me awake. I'm counting on a hot cup of coffee when you're done, though."

"That can be arranged."

"Maybe we should take that time to go over your blizzard preparedness, just in case."

"Fine with me. Coincidentally I made a grocery run after Caitlin left yesterday. When I heard about the storm on the weather channel I checked on my supply of candles and flashlights."

"And?"

"I'm good on that front, but is there more I should be doing? Should we string a rope line between the house and the barn so I can feed if I'm here by myself? I've heard stories about folks getting disoriented and becoming lost on their own property."

"We can string a line. Wouldn't hurt."

"Then let's do that today after it warms up a bit." She evaluated her job on the stall and called it good. "At first I thought I'd have the Christmas lights to guide me." She joined him in the aisle. "But then I realized if the power goes out…"

"No Christmas lights."

"Uh-huh." She snapped the pitchfork into a holder on the wall. "I was so close to buying a generator back in September. Maybe I should have."

"Made sense to wait. You don't have guests yet and the horses will be fine. You will, too. I just don't want you to run out of stuff to eat. Your stove is electric."

"As you've seen, I rarely use it, anyway. If I end up here by myself, I can eat your share of the sandwich fixings."

"Guess so."

"I also have my cheese and nuts, plus wine. You can tolerate suboptimal food if you pair it with a hearty red."

"You may be all set, then."

"Maybe, but I'll bet there are things I haven't thought of. Measures you'd take automatically." She put on her jacket and zipped it.

"Could be. I just thought of something. Let's bring in one of these shovels."

"I have a snow shovel at the house."

"I know, but one like this might be better if you have to tunnel out."

"*Tunnel out*?" She stared at him. "The snow could pile up so high I couldn't get out my front door?"

"Probably not. We only had to do that a couple of times, but—"

"By all means, let's take that shovel, then. The other one would be harder to maneuver if I had to dig my way…wait a minute. If you open the front door and there's a wall of snow, where do you put the snow you're shoveling?"

"We used the bathtub."

"Good Lord."

"The drift might not be that thick. You could potentially break through sooner than you think."

"Even so." She lifted a galvanized tub off a hook on the wall. "I'm taking this, too."

"That's not a bad idea. If the water pump stops working, you can melt snow in it."

"So I could be without water, too?"

"Probably not, but it's possible in a power outage. Ready?"

"For now. I'm glad we're going over this. I never dreamed I could end up with no running water and the front door blocked with snow. I can't just let it melt because I'll need to feed the horses."

"Yes, ma'am."

She followed him out of the barn and waited while he slid the bar across. "Maybe it'll be a polite snow, like we get in the mountains near San Francisco."

He grinned. "Don't count on it. You're in the Rockies, now. Our weather tends to be bigger and bolder than that."

She shivered, and not because of the temperature. Pete's jaunty smile sent fire racing through her veins. The weather wasn't the only big and bold element in her world.

15

Pete battled his protective instincts as he sat at Taryn's kitchen table drinking coffee and pretending that he wasn't the least bit worried. His concern wasn't logical. Even if they had the storm of the century, she could handle it. She was smart and resourceful.

Yes, she'd be alone out here, but she wasn't *that* far away. If she ended up in trouble, he'd get to her somehow. He glanced at his phone lying near hers on the table. His was fully charged. He'd make sure hers was, too.

Then again, she'd never used a rope line to get from the house to the barn. If she lost her footing and let go of the line, she could still get caught in a whiteout with no clue which way to go. What if—

"Have you ever done that?"

He glanced up. What had she been talking about? He had no clue. "Could you run it by me again?"

"I asked what you thought about using the fireplace to cook something, or at least heat water for a sponge bath."

"I'm sure you could in a pinch. I'll split more firewood today so you'll have plenty. We could figure out a place to store it in the house."

"The laundry room might work." She gazed at him. "You're worried about me, aren't you?"

"Not really."

"Yes, really. A moment ago you were staring into your coffee mug and scowling. Since there's no reason for you to be angry, it's gotta be worry. About me."

How to answer? If he told the truth, he'd reveal more than he cared to. His fears were more his problem than hers. He was fighting a primitive urge to stand guard against any threat to her safety, no matter how unlikely that threat might be.

"I will be okay," she said. "After talking it over with you, I'm convinced of it. We can string that line so I can get to the barn if visibility is poor. I'll have plenty of firewood. I can melt snow if I run out of water. I might be inconvenienced, but my life won't be in danger. Am I wrong about that? Is there something you're not telling me?"

"No. You're right. You'll be fine."

"I'm tougher than I look."

"I know." But her comment made him smile because her outward appearance was the opposite of tough. She was all soft skin and tempting curves. Someone might be fooled if they missed the glint of steel in her eyes.

"Speaking of firewood, if you'll split it, I'll clear a space in the laundry room and stack it there."

"You've got a deal. Let's get on that." He polished off his coffee.

"I'll check the weather app. If it's coming in sooner than expected, we need to hustle." She picked up her phone.

"Is your battery charged?"

"It is, but thanks for the reminder." After tapping the screen, she peered at it and began to laugh.

"What?"

"Now they're saying we *might* get a couple of inches."

"Well, damn. Talk about a letdown."

"I know! Epic anticlimax. I was so looking forward to lugging snow to the bathtub so I could tunnel my way out the front door. Oh, well." She laid her phone aside. "Back to our regularly scheduled program."

"Did you ever go through the pictures from yesterday?"

She gave him a startled glance then looked away. "Briefly. Not much there. Tell you what, let's take care of that wood while it's on our minds." Pushing back her chair, she stood.

"We can do that." Getting to his feet, he took their mugs to the sink. "You'll probably want to clear out those pictures before Saturday. Between Josh sitting on Santa's lap and the talent show, you'll need room on there."

"Good point. Why don't I just delete them?" She grabbed her phone.

"I'd like to take a look first, if you don't mind."

"Like I said, not much to see."

He doubted that. She was nervous as a cat in a room full of rocking chairs. He kept his voice casual. "I'm just curious. I've never seen a picture of me kissing someone." He held her gaze. "It's probably good for a laugh."

"I suppose so. Go for it." She handed him the phone. "I'll start shifting some things around in the laundry room to make room for the wood."

"Okay." He opened her pictures app. Whoa. Steamy. He scrolled through the shots while she clattered around in the laundry room making a fair amount of noise.

Huh. If he went faster, it was almost a video. A very hot video. Oh, baby. His groin tightened as he rapidly swiped his finger across the screen.

He'd been into that kiss. *She'd* been into that kiss, too. Had she ever. That moment when he'd slid his tongue inside and she'd opened for him…and that was the last picture. Damn it.

He stared at the final image, heart thumping, body taut. Other than the beat of his heart, it was very quiet. The noise in the laundry room had stopped. He glanced up from the screen.

She stood in the doorway of the laundry room, her color high, her breasts rising and falling with her rapid breathing. "Can I delete them, now?"

He sucked in air. "Um—"

"No reason to keep them, right?"

"Can't—" He cleared his throat. "Can't think of one." *Can't think of anything but kissing you. Again. And again.*

"Then I'll ditch them." She walked in and held out her hand.

If he took her hand and drew her into his arms, would she go along with that? He searched her gaze. *Desire. Confusion. Anxiety.*

That last one cast the deciding vote. He gave her the phone. "I'll go set up a timer for the lights and then I'll chop some wood." He left the kitchen quickly, snatched up his jacket and hat, and made tracks for the barn. He'd stored the leftover electric supplies there.

He grabbed a timer, his work gloves and the long-handled axe. After installing the timer, he headed for the woodpile behind the house.

Thank God for chores like this. He placed a thick piece of wood on the chopping block, swung the axe and split it cleanly in two. Nothing complicated about that.

He chose another heavy chunk, balanced it on the stump and swung the axe. Soon he'd found a soothing rhythm and his muscles warmed up. The tightness in his shoulders eased and the clean scent of wood shavings improved his mood.

Clouds drifted in, light gray. Snow clouds. The temperature dropped some, but by now he'd worked up a sweat. He peeled off his jacket and hooked it on a tree where a lower branch had broken off, leaving a perfect spot to hang stuff.

His arms ached, but that was a hell of a lot better than standing in that kitchen aching for Taryn. His uncle's comment last night about steering clear had sobered him. A wise man listened to hard-earned advice.

Trouble was, the minute he came within five feet of that woman, he became stupid as a box of rocks. He did dumb things like putting his arm around her to point out the issue with the lights. Then he'd insisted on seeing those kissing pictures.

Well, curiosity, or whatever damn-fool thing had been driving him, had resulted in sexual frustration such as he hadn't experienced in years. He'd bet money that she shared his frustration, but that didn't help. Made it worse, in fact.

"That's probably enough." She came out the back door, a log carrier in one hand. "I can't fit more than that in the laundry room."

He leaned on the axe handle and watched her walk toward him. A stiff breeze caught the edge of her hood, flinging it off and ruffling her hair. She didn't bother to pull it up again.

Her hair was the color of Clifford's coat. Funny that he'd never made that connection before. Could be why he admired it so much, although she might not appreciate the comparison. Then again, she might get a kick out of hearing it if they weren't both jacked up about those pictures.

He'd never had his hands in her hair, or cupped the back of her neck, or slid his arm around her narrow waist. He wanted all that and more. "Then I'll help you carry." Burying the axe blade in the stump, he went to fetch his jacket.

"I moved some cleaning supplies and laid down a tarp. Next spring I'll hire someone to add on a covered back porch so I can keep extra wood there."

"Good idea." He put on his jacket and loaded up his arms with wood while she filled her log carrier.

"Smells great out here."

"One of the perks of chopping wood." He followed her up the steps and through the door into the laundry room. "Smells good in here, too."

"I threw in a load of sheets. Figured if there was any chance the power would go out, I wanted clean sheets on my bed."

"Right." His response came out a little more clipped than he would have liked.

Her breath caught. "Poor choice of topic."

"It's fine." He waited for her to stack her wood in the area she'd designated, in a corner by the door into the kitchen.

The laundry room was narrow, so when she finished, she moved into the kitchen rather than trying to maneuver around him to go out the back door. Normally she would have edged past without worrying about the body contact.

He took his time stacking his armload of wood to see if she'd go out the front door and walk around the house to the wood pile. That would have been silly, but so was hovering by the doorway as he unloaded what he'd brought in.

After he placed the last log on the pile, he turned to her. "I could use another cup of coffee if you wouldn't mind making some."

She blinked in obvious surprise. "Sure." Taking off her parka, she hung it on the back of a kitchen chair before going over to the counter to start the coffee. "Do you want something to eat, too? It's nearly lunchtime. I could—"

"No, thanks. Just a cup of coffee is fine." He draped his jacket over the back of the chair he'd occupied earlier and laid his hat brim-side up on the table. "Will you have one with me?"

"I'd better not. I'm feeling a little wired." She turned on the electric grinder.

So was he, but sharing a cup of coffee was one way to initiate a conversation. He waited until the grinder stopped. "Never mind about the coffee, then. It was just an excuse. I was hoping we could sit down and have a discussion."

Her movements stilled. Slowly she faced him. "I think I knew that."

"And you'd rather not discuss anything?"

She took a deep breath and crossed her arms protectively over her chest. "I was willing to postpone it for a while, but since you're clearly ready, let's talk."

"Okay." He hated that she felt it necessary to assume that posture, as if his very presence was agitating her. He didn't know what to do about it. Her presence agitated him, too. "I love this job."

She nodded. "You're the perfect person for it. Kendra told me you would be and you are."

"I appreciate hearing that." He tucked his hands in his pockets. "Kissing you yesterday was pure pleasure, but it appears to have mucked up our working relationship."

"It wasn't just the kiss." She swallowed. "It was the pictures. I've deleted them, but…"

"Can't delete them from our brains, can we?"

"No."

"Which leaves us with a situation where we can't efficiently handle a simple task like transferring firewood into your laundry room. There was room for you to move past me and go out the back door to get another load. That would have saved time."

"I know. I didn't feel comfortable doing it. But that's my issue. I'll work on it. You make an excellent point about efficiency. While it isn't super important today, it will be as we go forward."

"I agree. One of our strengths is how well we're able to coordinate our efforts, no matter what we're doing. We're a good fit." No sooner had he used that phrase than he wanted it back.

Heat flickered in her eyes and then disappeared. "I made the decision to wait for you instead of squeezing past, but what if I hadn't? Would that have made you uncomfortable?"

Her body pressed against his, even for a split second? Oh, yeah. Even now, the possibility made his pulse race. "It would have affected me. But like you said, that's my issue. I'll work on it."

"Then I guess that's where we are. If we want to continue this mutually beneficial relationship, we both have some reprogramming to do. I'm willing to make that effort. Are you?"

"Absolutely." And it could be the toughest assignment he'd ever had in his life.

<u>16</u>

Taryn was committed to the new regime, but she didn't care to test it quite yet. Thanks to her discussion with Pete, it was officially lunchtime, so she chose to fix them some food and hot tea while he brought in the rest of the wood.

Darkening skies and a wind whipping the branches of the spruce trees out in the front yard prompted her to build a fire. Then she turned on a couple of lamps and the Christmas tree lights.

She set up their meal at the game table instead of the coffee table, though. Not as cozy, and they could see the fire but also keep an eye on the weather through the picture window.

Pete finished bringing in the wood and washed up at the kitchen sink as he always did. Usually she chatted with him while he did that, but today she went into the living room to check the fire.

Maybe tomorrow she'd be better able to share the kitchen with his manly self when he rolled back his sleeves and lathered up. Given another twenty-four hours to recalibrate, she might not notice the golden blond hair sprinkled over his forearms, or the supple motion of his fingers as he worked the suds between them and over the backs of his hands.

"You have a text," he called from the kitchen.

"Would you please check to see if it's from Caitlin?" She used the tongs to reposition a log that hadn't caught. "She promised to send me something by midday."

"It's from her. She's sent you some stills and videos."

"Great." Especially since looking at that would give them something to focus on during lunch. Without a distraction, they might eat in uncomfortable silence.

That had never happened before. Topics had always been easy to find. "I'll get my laptop and we can go through them while we eat." She retrieved her laptop from the bedroom she'd had remodeled into an office.

"This'll be exciting." Pete came into the living room with the aroma of her kitchen soap, a pine-scented one, clinging to his hands and forearms. He hadn't bothered to roll his sleeves down.

Not as exciting as you, buster. She gave herself a mental slap upside the head. She wasn't supposed to be evaluating him on her personal excite-o-meter. "I can't wait to see Crimson Clouds through her eyes."

"Same here, and I'm glad to report that our decorations are standing up to this wind."

"That's good news."

"That's why I wanted to wire the heck out of every branch. I'm not ready to feed them to the blizzard gods."

"Except we're not having a visit from the blizzard gods. I'm still a little disappointed about that."

"Stick around this area and you'll get your blizzard fix sooner or later." He waited for her to sit down before pulling out a chair. "I'm just as glad it's not coming in now. A couple of inches will make it look like Christmas and everyone's holiday lights won't be knocked out."

"You want my polite snow?"

"Pretty much."

She pushed her sandwich plate to one side for the time being, opened her laptop and called up her email. "I kind of wish we'd had polite snow on the ground for Caitlin's pictures."

"Must be hard to plan that kind of thing. Caitlin has a schedule and the snow doesn't."

"And I have a schedule." She waited for the first video to download. "I'd like to get the Christmas package on the website in the next day or two."

"Then be glad there was no blizzard to wrestle with. That would put a hitch in your online giddy-up."

She glanced across the table and smiled. "Yes, it would. Hey, go ahead and start eating."

"Waiting for you."

"Thank you." The video downloaded and she swiveled the laptop so they could both see it. "This is the one she took after you left yesterday, when the lights came on."

Ignoring his sandwich, he turned to face the screen as the video began. Caitlin had used an instrumental of *Winter Wonderland* as the musical backdrop and filmed the lighted decorations in such a way that snow was suggested, if not visible.

When it ended, Pete sat back in his chair. "I'll be damned. You'd swear there was snow covering the ground even if there were only those little patches here and there."

"She has talent." She glanced at his untouched sandwich. "Looks like neither one of us can multitask when it comes to something like this. Let's eat and then watch the rest."

"I'm not good at multitasking, period. I have a one-track mind."

She laughed. Couldn't help it.

"I didn't mean that the way it sounded."

"I'm sure you didn't." She picked up her mug of tea, took a cautious sip and put it down again. "Watch that tea. It's hot."

"Just how I like it." Then he heaved a sigh and swore under his breath.

"Problem?"

He met her gaze. "It seems I *do* have a one-track mind."

Her stomach fluttered. "Understandable. This might take some time."

He nodded.

"We have to override a natural attraction. If we'd met under different circumstances…"

"I've thought of that. Like maybe I'd already taken a job somewhere and you'd hired a different foreman." He picked up his sandwich. "A guy in his sixties."

"Why in his sixties?"

"Wouldn't want someone who could be competition." He took a bite of his sandwich.

"I see." She started eating.

"Then some night we would've both ended up at the Guzzling Grizzly, each of us out with friends. I'd ask you to dance."

"You dance?"

"Yes, ma'am."

"Something I didn't know."

He finished chewing and swallowed. "No reason to. We've never been at the GG together in the evening. Anyway, I'd notice you sitting there and ask you to dance."

"Why would you notice me?"

"The color of your hair. I'm partial to it."

"You've dated a lot of redheads?"

"Not really. Come to think of it, not any. But your hair is the exact same color as..." He shook his head. "Never mind."

"What? The sunset? Your favorite amber beer? Rusty pipes?"

He smiled. "It's best if I don't say. Not sure whether you'd feel complimented. What's amazing is that I didn't think of the similarity until today, when you came out to get the firewood."

"If you're going to tell me that my hair looks like flames, I've heard that one before. Several times, in fact."

"That's not it. Given that you've spent your life in San Francisco, I doubt anyone has ever made this particular comparison."

"My curiosity is killing me."

He hesitated.

"Come on. After all this buildup, you have to tell me."

"Your hair is the same color as my horse Clifford."

She started giggling.

"It's why he has that name, because of the big red dog in the kid's book."

She nodded and pressed her napkin to her mouth to hold back the giggles that kept coming. Her hair matched his horse's coat. Most adorable compliment ever.

"But the dog in that book is lipstick red. Clifford is a rich auburn color, just like yours. His coat is amazing, especially after I finish grooming him."

She used her napkin to wipe away tears of laughter. "I'd love—" She stopped to clear her throat. "I'd love to meet him sometime."

"Seems odd that you never have, but it makes sense. You were gone for both holidays when we had a parade. Maybe that's why I didn't realize the color thing. I've never seen the two of you together. He's a great horse. Had him since I turned sixteen."

"Is he old, then?"

"He's twenty. I know there are folks who consider that an old horse, but it's not. They can live to be forty if you treat 'em right."

"Maybe on Christmas Day we could pay him a visit since I'll be at Wild Creek."

"We'll do that. He'd really..." The wind howled outside and his attention shifted to the window. "It sure is kicking up out there. Want to check the weather on your computer to be sure nothing's changed?"

"I'm on it." She pulled the laptop closer and accessed her favorite weather channel. "It's taking its time loading."

"Could be plenty of other folks are trying to get the same info."

"Could be. Ah, here it comes. It's…uh, oh."

"What?"

She turned the screen so he could see it. "I'm not from here, but that looks—"

"Serious. It is." He pushed back from the table. "Let's get the horses inside."

"My parka's in the kitchen." She hurried to get it. "How much time do we have?"

"Hard to predict, but the way that wind's blowing, it could be soon. Fingers crossed we'll be able to string that line. Looks like you may need it."

Adrenaline shot through her as she shoved her arms in the sleeves of her parka and zipped it. Frigid air swept into the house when Pete opened the front door and she dashed out on the porch and down the steps. He was right behind her, taking them two at a time.

She tightened the cord on her hood and tied it under her chin, but fingers of wind flung it back, anyway. To hell with it. She put on the gloves she'd left in her pockets after hauling wood. "At least it's not snowing yet." Her words were ripped away by the wind. Pete likely hadn't heard her. And no sooner had she said it than the clouds began spitting snow.

Their little herd of six was huddled near the gate, clearly hoping the humans would show up. A fierce protective urge rose within her. Pete had said the horses could weather a storm better than a person, but she wanted them in that barn ASAP.

Pete's voice rose above the wind. "I'm not gonna mess with lead ropes. I'll just grab their halters. I can take two of 'em. Think you can take one more and then close the gate?"

"Yep!" She jogged in place to keep warm as he unlatched the gate, went in and grabbed Spike's halter in one hand and Marley's in the other. He led them out the gate and she slipped inside.

"Here we g-go, Honey B-Butter." Teeth chattering from the cold, she got a firm hold on the palomino's halter, led him out and latched the gate behind her. She met Pete coming back to the pasture.

"Once you get him in his stall, come back to the door. I'll be there with the other three."

"Got it." She had no idea how he'd do that but he was the boss of this maneuver. Snow pelted her hard in the face. Felt almost like little rocks. Hail?

Pete had left the door open. Yay. The warmth of the barn enveloped her in a hug but Honey Butter shook himself, spraying her with melted snow. "Oh, well. That's water I won't need to towel off you later, buddy." She closed him quickly in his stall and jogged back to the barn entrance.

Pete came toward her riding bareback on Fifty Shades while leading Buster on one side and Junior on the other. Snow was collecting on his hat and the shoulders of his shearling coat. He'd ducked his head to block the wind blasting him in the face.

He lifted his head when he drew close to the barn. "Take Junior. I'll get the other two."

She reached for the horse on Pete's right. "I've got him. You can let go."

Unclamping his fingers from the halter, he slid off Fifty Shades, grabbed the dappled gray's halter, and led both horses inside the barn. Minutes later, all six geldings were in their stalls and the barn door was closed. Wind whistled through the cracks.

"Now what?" Taryn unzipped her parka, which had become too warm. Her hair that Pete so admired was plastered to her head.

"We need to fetch a couple of scrapers and get the worst of the water out of their coats." Pete unbuttoned his jacket and took off his hat, tapping it against his thigh to knock off the excess moisture.

"And then?"

"Feed them, even though it's a little early. Without a rope running to the house, we might have trouble getting down here later."

"No rope, then?"

He shook his head. "Can't install one when it's like this. And whiteouts are a distinct possibility. As are power outages. We need to get back to the house while the power's still on and we can see the living room lights from here."

She took a deep breath. "Guess this isn't a very polite snow."

He smiled. "No, ma'am."

"But if we feed the horses now, then maybe the worst of it will be over by morning and I can—"

"I'm not leaving you."

She blinked. "What?"

"I realize it will be awkward, especially after the past couple of days, but this is shaping up to be a monster storm. I'm not leaving you to deal with it alone."

Her heartbeat thundered in her ears. Whoops, now she could barely breathe. "You're…staying? Through the night?"

"It's not safe for you to be here by yourself." A gust of wind rattled the barn doors as if to underscore his statement.

"Oh." Her brain refused to work at all, but her body was throwing a wild party, alternating between heat waves and cold chills.

Maybe he'd draw a line in the sand by announcing that he'd sleep on the couch. He didn't do that.

Alternatively, she could inform him that's where he'd sleep. She didn't do that, either.

Instead she met his steady gaze. "Should be interesting."

<u>17</u>

Pete hadn't made the decision lightly. If he'd had another choice, he would have taken it. Maybe he and Taryn could be snowbound for hours together without giving in to temptation, but he doubted it.

Promising to stay clear of her was setting himself up to be dishonorable. He had excellent self-restraint but he was only half the picture. She hadn't made any promises, either, likely for the same reason he hadn't.

He finished using the scraper on Marley's bourbon-colored coat and dried the gelding's face with a towel while telling him what a good boy he was. Taryn was two stalls down doing the same with Fifty Shades. She'd talked to each of the horses she'd worked on, but hadn't directed any comments to him.

Just as well. This wasn't the time for small talk. The storm continued to batter the old wooden barn, but it was a sturdy structure. He'd made sure of that before bringing any horses into it.

He finished up when Taryn did and they automatically moved into their feeding routine. Delivering hay flakes took no time at all.

He stowed his wheelbarrow and met her at the front of the barn. "This is it." He reached for the jackets they'd hung on the wall. "We need to hold onto each other on the way back to the house. Visibility is likely much worse than when we came down here. It's easy to lose track of someone."

She nodded. "Understood."

He buttoned his coat, crammed his hat on his head and put on his gloves. Then he waited while she tightened the cord holding her hood in place and pulled on her gloves. "Ready?"

"Let's do it."

He coughed. "Um, okay."

"Just an expression." A gleam of mischief flashed in her eyes.

"I knew that." His heart was still racing, though. He took a steadying breath. "I'll have to close the barn door once we're out there. I'll go out first. I want you to grab the back of my jacket with both hands, follow me out, and hold tight to the jacket while I close the door."

"Roger that." She gave him a little smile and a quick salute.

"I don't mean to sound like a drill sergeant. But I—"

Her expression softened. "You want us to be safe. I know, and I appreciate it. I'm not making fun, just trying to lighten the mood."

And now that she had, he wanted to kiss her. Bad time for that activity. "Let's go." He unfastened the hooks holding the door. "Grab hold."

"Gotcha."

The tug on his jacket told him she'd followed his instructions. Opening the door only enough so his shoulders would clear, he gave an involuntary gasp. Damn, it was *cold*.

Her boots crunched on the snow as she came out. While he slid the door back into place, she moved behind him, hanging on exactly as he'd instructed. He shoved the bar across and turned, reaching for her. "Put your arm around my waist."

She snuggled against him as he pulled her in close, which wasn't easy with the slippery material of the parka. Then he faced in the direction of the house.

Snow eddied and swirled, confusing his sense of direction. Where was the damn house? He glanced over his shoulder at the barn to orient himself. Okay. The house should be right…a faint light glowed and was gone, obscured by a shifting curtain of snow.

He moved forward a few steps and paused, waiting for another rift, another glimpse of that light.

"Can you see the house?" Taryn's voice wavered. Not much, but enough to betray her alarm.

"Not right this minute. Waiting for the light to show up again. There!" He surged forward, propelling her along with him. Got at least a dozen steps closer before he lost sight of that beacon.

"I get that rope thing."

"Makes it a lot easier."

"How soon before the Christmas lights come on?"

"Not sure. I think soon. That would help." He tightened his grip as Taryn began to shiver. "Hang on. We just need to make sure we're heading in the right—ah!" Light filtered through again and he took several more steps toward it before the wind-whipped snow wiped out the faint glimmer.

"Aren't we close enough? Can't we just keep going in that direction?"

"Not a good idea."

"Should've b-brought my phone. It has a c-compass."

"Wouldn't work. Too cold. We just have to—hallelujah!" The outdoor lights flashed on. Hundreds of tiny bulbs sparkled in the darkness, showing him the way home. He blessed every single one.

He maintained his hold on Taryn because the wind hadn't let up at all. Clamping his free hand on his hat, he plowed ahead. The wind buffeted them constantly until they finally reached the shelter of the porch.

Letting go, he gulped for air and gestured toward the door. "After you." He followed her through the door into warmth and safety, closed the door and sighed.

She faced him, her chest heaving. "Let's...never do...that again."

"Yeah, let's not." He held her gaze, tried to get his footing. Now that the immediate danger was over, he was no longer the one in charge. Her house. Her rules.

She dragged in another breath. "I had no idea it would get so...intense."

"Next time you'll have a rope line."

"You know it. Thank you for getting us back safely."

"You're welcome." Evidently she wasn't going to throw herself into his arms out of gratitude or she would have done that already.

Breaking eye contact, she glanced down at the polished wood floor where puddles were forming around each of them. "Let's move this party to the kitchen, or better yet, the laundry room."

"Good plan. I left my phone in the kitchen. I need to call my dad." He followed her, sticking to the same path she made so the water would be contained as much as possible. "The rope line, by the way, will run from the barn to your back door, so you can avoid this kind of mess in the main part of the house."

"That's sensible."

"It'll be up before the next storm." Good thing he wasn't in the habit of crying over spilled milk or he'd be lecturing himself for not taking immediate action this morning.

"Considering what we've just been through, water on the floor is a minor detail. We're fine and the horses are fine. That's all that matters."

"I agree." He took off his gloves and held onto them while he picked up his phone from the kitchen table. A text from his dad was on the screen.

Walking into the laundry room, he breathed in the fragrant cedar stacked in the corner. At least the wood supply had been taken care of. "I'm going to call my dad." He laid his hat and gloves on top of the industrial-sized dryer and unbuttoned his jacket. "He's already texted me wanting to know if we're okay."

"By all means." She took off her parka and put it on a hanger. "Give me your jacket and I'll hang it up to dry."

He handed it over. "Thanks." Her hair was tangled and damp from getting snowed on earlier. He'd never seen it that disheveled, as if she'd come out of the shower, grabbed a towel and rubbed it over her wet hair.

A shower would feel great right now. His clothes were wet and clammy. She might be in the same fix. If she'd be willing to join him in the shower...

Oh, hell, he was getting *way* ahead of himself. No telling how tonight would go, and even if they turned up the heat, certain activities were off the table. He hadn't anticipated this eventuality. But they could have a whole lot of fun playing around in the shower...

The laundry room grew smaller, more intimate. His body tightened. He'd better get the hell out of there. He quickly pulled off his boots. "Got a couple of old towels? I'll wipe up the floor while I make the call."

"Sure. Here you go." She pulled two out of a canvas bag hanging on the wall.

He took the frayed towels. "I'll build up the fire, too," he said over his shoulder as he fled.

"Then I'll make us some hot tea," she called after him.

"Great!" He didn't need hot tea. Too bad he couldn't take a detour outside. Stepping barefoot onto the porch would take his mind off warm showers and wet, naked bodies. He'd been alone in the house with her for less than ten minutes and he was already bolloxed up.

He walked toward the front door, rolling his shoulders to ease the tension. After dropping both towels onto the puddles, he called his dad, who answered right away.

"Where are you, son?"

"Safe and warm in Taryn's living room." He stepped on the towels and moved them around with his feet. "Where are you?"

"Safe and warm in my living room."

"With Kendra?"

"Nope. The blizzard came up so fast we got caught on opposite sides of the road. I'll be spending the evening with your favorite uncle, who—"

"I'm his only uncle! But I'd be your favorite even if you had ten others in the queue, right, mate?"

"Absolutely, Uncle Brendan."

"He asked me to put your call on speaker, in case you haven't figured that out."

"'Course I asked to be on the call! Had to hear it straight from the horse's mouth that my nephew's all right. Damn sneaky blizzard. Happy to know you're not out in it."

"Nobody should be out in it," his dad said. "I advise you to stay put."

"I planned on it, Dad." When the area by the door was fairly dry, he skated over the wet footprints leading to the kitchen. "How about everybody else? Who've you talked to?"

"All three. You were the only one left. The GG closed early so Michael and Roxanne are tucked into their new house with plenty of supplies. Wes cancelled his appointments and he's with Ingrid. Their building has a generator so the bakery won't lose power. Gage, Emma and Josh are safe and secure at Gage's house. Kendra's brood is all accounted for, too."

"That's good to hear." He reached the kitchen doorway. The teakettle on the stove was whistling and Taryn was finger-combing her hair, her back to him. He picked up the towels and retreated.

"Impressive crisis management," his uncle said. "When the zombie apocalypse hits, I'll be on the first flight over here."

"Zombies are even more unpredictable than blizzards," Pete said. "Better make that move now." He crossed to the fireplace where a few embers still glowed.

"That's what your dad says. He misses me."

"Yeah." His dad chuckled. "Even if you are a pain in the ass. So, Pete, is everything copasetic over there? When I didn't hear back from you right away, I—"

"Had some trouble getting back to the house from the barn just now." He dropped the towels on the hearth and moved the screen. "No rope line."

"Ah. Bet you'll have one set up next time."

"Oh, yeah." He stirred the embers and added kindling. "I'll be all over that when the weather clears." The kindling caught and he put on a medium-sized log.

"But you made it through, despite that. I take it her critters are fed?"

"Yep. They should be fine until tomorrow."

"How about you?"

"We have plenty of firewood, enough food for now, a shovel, flashlights, lanterns and batteries. I think we're set."

"That's good," his dad said. "I—"

"Hey, mate, sounds like a cozy situation you got, there."

"I guess you could say that, Uncle Brendan."

"See, the thing is, I'm slightly worried that you'll—"

"Don't be, Brendan," his dad said. "Pete will be fine."

"If you say so, big brother."

"I do. Have a good night, son."

"Thanks, Dad."

"Don't do anything I wouldn't do," his uncle added with a laugh right before his dad disconnected the call.

What the hell was he supposed to make of *that*? If he interpreted the various comments correctly, his dad was subtly giving his blessing and Uncle Brendan was sending warning signals.

After replacing the fireplace screen, he picked up the towels and walked back into the kitchen.

Taryn finished pouring tea into one of the two mugs on the counter and gave him a quick glance. "You can put those on top of the dryer. And thanks for doing that."

"You bet." He got rid of the towels and walked back in.

"Everything all right with your dad?" She set the teapot aside.

Judging from the spicy aroma, they'd be drinking the same cinnamon blend they'd had for lunch. Seemed like hours ago. "He's fine. Everybody's checked in and Kendra's been in contact with her kids, too. They're all accounted for."

"Good." She gestured toward the mugs. "Tea's ready. If you'll take it in by the fire, I'll get my laptop and work on uploading Caitlin's video to the website since we still have power."

He picked up both mugs. "I stoked the fire just now."

"Thought I heard you doing that. The bakery was closed when I went into town for a few groceries yesterday, so I bought a package of chocolate fudge cookies. Want some?"

"Sure do." He'd take whatever she offered—including a night in her arms. If that turned out to be the worst mistake of his life, so be it.

18

Tea, cookies and working on her laptop. Wasn't this wholesome? Concentrating wasn't easy while sharing the couch with a virile cowboy who'd heroically guided them through a blizzard, but Taryn managed to upload the video and an announcement of next year's Christmas getaway.

"That's enough for now." She shut down her laptop and set it on a small end table next to her empty mug.

Pete took another cookie from the package sitting between them. If they'd left them on the coffee table, heat from the fire might have melted the chocolate frosting. Amazing that they hadn't melted sitting between her and Pete.

"I'm glad you got something up there." He bit into the cookie.

"I am, too." She helped herself to another cookie. Chocolate was a poor substitute for what she craved, but a safer option. If Pete scooped her up and hauled her back to the bedroom, she doubted her ability to resist.

He didn't. Instead he ate cookies and tended the fire as if sex was the last thing on his mind. That couldn't be right, not after the way he'd reacted to those pictures of their kiss.

Would they avoid the subject all evening? Would she eventually hand him a pillow and blankets so he could make a bed on the couch while she slept alone in her roomy king?

That was assuming the power stayed on. If it didn't, she'd be right here with him next to the fireplace. They'd need to keep each other warm, share body heat. Game over.

He got up to tend the fire. Impossible to ignore the sheer masculine beauty of him as he grasped the tongs with his capable hands. From his first day on the job, she'd been fascinated by the skillful way he knotted a rope or effortlessly slipped on a bridle. Fascinated and aroused. She'd denied the attraction.

He could dance. Didn't surprise her. He rode a horse with a natural rhythm that stirred her blood. His guidance had turned her into a decent rider, but she might never achieve his ease in the saddle. A sexy nonchalance settled over him like a superhero's cloak when he mounted up.

She'd been alone with him countless times in the seven months since he'd come to work for her. But never like this. The barriers had been partially destroyed by their hot kiss. Today the force of a shared crisis had knocked down the bulk of her defenses. The blizzard's muscular winds would have brought her to her knees if not for his steady grip.

Not all the barriers had disappeared, though. If they sat here long enough making pleasant conversation, they might succeed in rebuilding the walls between them. It was the sensible course of action. The safest path.

What to do? She didn't know, damn it! And she couldn't keep sitting there, pretending she didn't want...everything he had to offer.

She couldn't have everything, though. He wouldn't be prepared for that. Not his style. But there were alternatives. Did she have the courage to make the first move?

Exhaling an impatient breath, she stood. "I'm desperate for a shower, but it seems unfair for me to get comfy when you don't have a change of clothes."

He set the tongs in their stand and replaced the fireplace screen. "Got a blanket I could borrow?"

She stared at him as the implications of that exploded like firecrackers in her brain. "You'd be okay wrapping up in a blanket?" *Naked*?

"Compared to sitting around the rest of the night in what I have on? You betcha. Water ran down my collar so my t-shirt got wet. Not pleasant then and less pleasant now. As for my jeans—well, they're in the same condition as yours."

"Clammy and icky."

"Pretty much. Thanks to the fire, the denim below my knees is drying, but just the front. I've made sure only the dry part of me touches the couch cushions, which is less than relaxing."

"I could put your stuff through the washer and dryer. In fact, I should do that ASAP in case the power goes out, but...a blanket? Are you sure?"

"It would be a huge relief to get out of these clothes and into a warm shower." He hesitated. "But if the blanket plan would make you uncomfortable, then—"

"If you're fine with it, I'm fine with it."

"I don't claim to be the most modest guy in the world. Used to go skinny dipping all the time when I lived on the Lazy S."

"Not here?"

"Not yet." He grinned. "My boss has kept me busy."

"Then follow me. I'll get you set up in the guest bathroom." She led the way down the hall and flipped the wall switch to light up the bathroom located across from her office. Taking inventory, she came back out. "You've got soap and even a bottle of shampoo if you want to wash your hair. Plenty of towels, too."

"Awesome. Thank you."

"I'll wait here. Toss your clothes out the door when you're undressed and I'll start the washer before I take my shower."

"Alrighty." He walked into the bathroom and pushed the door almost closed. "I just thought of something." Snaps popped as he took off his shirt. "I was planning to help you fix dinner, whatever that turns out to be." His belt buckle clinked as it hit the tile floor. "If I'm wearing a blanket I could be a hazard in the kitchen."

"No worries. I'll wait on you." Like this wasn't arousing, standing out here listening to him strip down.

"Here you go." He extended his bare, muscled arm through the opening and handed out a bundle of his clothes. "Appreciate it."

"No problem. Once I've started the washer, I'll get you a blanket and put it beside the door."

"Excellent. Thanks." He left the door slightly open. Water splashed into the tub and then spray hit the shower walls.

When he started humming Tim McGraw's *I Like It, I Love It* and slapping a washcloth against his skin, she gave herself a mental shake and hurried away from the door. *Get a grip, girlfriend.*

Laundry wisdom said she shouldn't wash his shirt, t-shirt, jeans and knit briefs together. Oh, and his socks, which he'd left on the dryer when he'd taken off his boots. But this was a special case. The intimate task required her to handle his soft knit briefs. Dark gray. His t-shirt was also soft and snowy white.

She lifted the shirt to her nose and closed her eyes. Such a familiar scent. She'd never consciously admitted that it turned her on.

After dumping soap in the dispenser, she was about to tap the Start button. Then she paused. Why not? Quickly taking off her clothes, she tossed them in with his and started the washer.

Although she had no neighbors, she'd never dashed naked through her house before. Again, why not? Pete's skinny dipping comment inspired her to risk it.

Hey, it was kinda fun! Liberating, even. She'd reached the hallway when he poked his head out the bathroom door.

His eyes widened.

She barreled past him. "Your blanket! Be right back with it!" She ducked into her bedroom.

"Love the streak!"

"Thanks!" She pressed a hand to her wildly beating heart. Whew. Bold move. And she would own it.

On the other hand, running around naked for no reason when there was a blizzard raging outside veered toward stupid. Grabbing her thick terry robe from its hook on her bathroom door, she put it on and quickly tied the sash. Then she threw back her comforter and pulled her favorite blanket off the bed.

After folding it, she walked down the hall with the blanket clutched in her arms. Her face was warm so she was probably blushing. Couldn't do anything about that.

He stood in the bathroom doorway with a towel tucked around his hips, his broad chest on display, his hair damp and a smile on his handsome face. "If it weren't so chilly, I could go with just the towel."

"You'd be cold." She handed him the blanket. "That's why I was running. Threw my clothes in with yours and took off."

His smile widened. "Figured that was the situation." He cradled the blanket against his chest. "Thanks for this. It feels as soft as the one you put on the bed in the honeymoon cabin."

"Same brand."

"Is this yours, then? The one you have on your bed?"

"Yes, it is, but don't worry about it. I—"

"I'm honored."

She blinked. "I thought you were about to turn it down and ask for a different one."

"Nope. I'm not that noble. If you're willing to let me use it until my clothes are dry, I accept. I'll bet wrapping myself in it will feel great."

"Oh, it will. Um, I mean—"

"You've curled up in it naked?"

"Maybe a time or two."

A gleam of amusement lit his gaze. "Taryn Maroney, you have hidden depths."

"Doesn't everyone?" She backed away. "I need to take my shower."

"Want help with that?"

Her pulse raced as she hesitated. Nope. Not that bold. "No thanks. I'll be out soon."

"Mind if I get us a couple of longnecks and some munchies?"

"Help yourself. At this point it's share and share alike."

"I like the sound of that."

She gave him a quick smile. "Yeah, me, too." Turning, she walked into her bedroom and shut the door. He'd seen her naked. She'd seen him semi-naked. No going back, now.

Nothing about this encounter was familiar. No romantic strolls, no flowers, no candlelit dinners. They might end up with that last experience if the power went out, but it would be unlike any candlelit dinner she'd ever had.

The wild weather had stranded them here and helped set the tone for...what? A romp. That's exactly where they were headed. She glanced at the digital clock on her bedside table. The night was still young. Bring it on.

19

Before getting out the beer, Pete checked to see when the wash would be done. Still twenty-eight minutes left. His phone lay on the kitchen table where he'd left it, so he set the timer.

Even factoring in the obvious advantage of going without clothes while sitting by the fire with Taryn, he chafed at the lack of mobility. Maneuvering while wrapped in Taryn's blanket was tricky.

He'd tripped a couple of times, and when he was fetching their beer he caught the blanket in the refrigerator door. Slicing up some cheese while trying to hold the blanket in place was a non-starter, too. He finally draped it over a kitchen chair so he wouldn't do damage to himself.

Chilly proposition, though, being naked in this weather. The house was heated and insulated, but blizzard-driven cold air had a way of seeping in anyway. His nipples tightened and his boys weren't happy, either.

Slinging the blanket over his shoulders like an oversized beach towel, he carried the beer and munchies into the living room. Tending the fire would have to be done au natural, too, or he'd likely catch the blanket on fire. Leaving it on the couch, he redistributed the charred pieces and added another log from the supply in a wrought iron holder near the fireplace. That done, he wrapped up again and sat down.

The blanket was even softer than the one he'd help Taryn put on the honeymoon bed. He might have to look into getting one. Knowing this belonged to Taryn and that she'd snuggled naked in it made the experience even more arousing. The blanket was generously sized and could easily accommodate two.

That little streak of hers was a promising beginning to the evening. She clearly hadn't expected him to catch her. Yet she'd dared to do it when there was always a chance he would.

Thanks to good timing, he'd captured an unforgettable image of Taryn throwing caution to the winds. When he replayed the scene, his cock twitched. Maybe, just maybe, she was willing to live in the moment and let tomorrow take care of itself.

"The fire's looking good." She walked in wearing green plaid flannel pajamas and green velvet slippers. Not naked, but certainly not dressed, either. "Must be dicey working with hot coals when you're wearing a blanket."

"Which is why I didn't do it that way."

Her eyebrows lifted. "Now there's a visual."

"Yeah, you'd better take charge of the fire. One glimpse of my manly physique and you might go crazy."

"Do you get that a lot?" She settled down next to him on the couch, leaving about a foot between them.

"No, but I keep hoping." Holding the blanket in place, he handed her a beer and picked up the other one for himself.

She took a sip of her beer and turned to him, amusement and something more potent lighting up her dark eyes. "What sort of reaction are you looking for?"

"Oh, the usual. Gasping, swooning, that kind of thing."

She responded with a teasing smile. "If that's the criteria, I guess you didn't go crazy when you saw me naked."

"Oh, I went crazy." His attention drifted to her smiling mouth, so full, so tempting...

"Not that I could tell. When I came back with the blanket you were perfectly calm."

"That was an act. I was doing my best to convince you I'm super cool." His gaze lifted, locked with hers. "Still am."

"Trying to convince me you're cool or going crazy?"

"Both."

Her throat moved in a slow swallow. "That doesn't sound like an easy combination."

"It isn't. I may have to choose one or the other."

Her lips parted as she dragged in a breath. "Which one?"

He set his beer on the coffee table. The blanket slipped off his shoulder and he let it fall.

"Being cool is a lost cause when I'm wearing a blanket."

"But without it you'll get cold."

"Not if you come a little closer."

Slowly she put her beer on the coffee table and toed off her slippers. Then she got up, moved in front of him and climbed onto his lap. "Is that close enough?"

His heartbeat thundered in his ears. "Yes, ma'am. That'll...that'll do." Sliding his trembling fingers through her silky hair, he cupped the back of her head and applied gentle pressure until her breath tickled face. "That'll do just fine."

Her lips met his with an eagerness that sent throbbing heat straight to his package. Pushing the blanket off his other shoulder, she smoothed her hands over his tight muscles, caressing, kneading, stoking the fire.

Sliding his hand under her pajama top, he touched warm satin skin. She sighed when he cupped her breast, moaned when he flexed his fingers and...his phone alarm went off.

She eased away from the kiss. "Is that your phone?"

"Yes." He grasped the hem of her pajama top and pulled it over her head.

"Should we—"

"No." Cradling her breasts, he brushed his thumbs over her nipples.

Her eyes darkened as she gripped his shoulders and rose to her knees. Her voice, low and sultry, drifted on a sigh. "Okay." Closing her eyes, she leaned into his caress, inviting him to explore.

She tasted like…heaven. Supple and responsive, she rewarded him with whimpers and cries, digging her fingers into his shoulders as he licked and suckled. Her hips grew restless, creating sweet torture as the blanket caressed his privates. Couldn't take much more of that. And she was so ready to be loved.

Gathering her close, he guided her down to the plump cushions and followed her there as he nibbled his way from one quivering breast to the other. He threw off the blanket, which tumbled to the floor.

He lay half-on and half-off the couch. Aroused with no immediate relief in sight. Didn't matter. All that mattered was giving satisfaction to the woman lying beneath him, her hot body begging for what he could provide.

Her pajama bottoms slipped right off. Kissing his way down to the treasure he sought, he breathed in the scent of arousal. He blew softly on her damp curls and nuzzled her passion-slick inner thighs. She trembled when he slid his hands beneath her, holding and lifting her toward his mouth.

He touched down lightly at first. A flick of his tongue, a brush of his lips. Her breath caught. A deeper kiss. Firmer pressure with his tongue. A slow, insistent rhythm. She began to pant.

He feasted now, reveling in her uninhibited cries as she abandoned herself to him, urging him on as he took her higher, ever higher. Her thighs shook and she arched into his caress. Almost there…

And she came, laughing, shouting, jubilant beyond his wildest hopes for this moment. He stayed with her, easing her back to earth, bestowing kisses on her most private of places.

Firelight danced over her flushed skin as he retraced his path and gazed into her smiling eyes.

"Pete." Reaching up, she pushed away a lock of hair that had fallen over his forehead. "That was…"

"Awesome?"

"Beyond awesome."

"Glad you liked it."

"Loved it." She stroked his cheek. "Thank you."

"We're facing some limitations. I'm not in the habit of carting around—"

"I would've been shocked if you were."

He captured her hand and placed a kiss in her palm. "Would've come in handy tonight, though."

"We'll manage. I have some ideas, too, you know."

"Oh, really?" He managed to tame his cock, but that comment sabotaged his efforts. "What kind of ideas?"

"If you don't know, then tonight will be extremely educational for you."

"I'm looking forward to it." He sent a silent apology to his bad boy as he sat back on his heels. "But my phone was signaling that the wash is done. So I—"

"Wait a minute." She propped herself on her elbows. "What's your phone doing talking to my washing machine?"

"Before I got the beer and munchies I checked to see when the wash would be done and set the timer on my phone."

"Ah. You may be surprised to hear that I'd forgotten all about the laundry."

He smiled. "Good for my ego."

"You, however, are on top of this."

"Habit. Prioritizing the jobs that require electricity."

"Then let's throw those clothes in the dryer." She scooted off the couch.

"I'll help." He stood.

She paused, her gaze traveling slowly from head to toe. "Doing laundry may never be the same."

"Want me to stay here?"

"Are you kidding? You look like the statue of David only better endowed. Keep me company."

He laughed. "Glad to." He followed her into the laundry room. "Let me know if you're getting cold and I'll warm you up."

"I'm not the least bit cold. Are you?"

"No, ma'am. We may have discovered the perfect way to wait out a blizzard."

20

Standing naked in a laundry room transferring clothes from the washer to the dryer was a first for Taryn. Sharing the task with a muscular cowboy who was also naked was one for the record books.

Pete took clothes out of the washer and she tossed them in the dryer. "I wouldn't normally dry everything together, but this is an unusual circumstance."

"You think?" He dangled her black bra by the shoulder straps. "Sexy."

"Thanks." She draped it over the drying rack.

He held up the matching panties. "Do your undies dry fast?"

"Probably not in this weather." She put those on the rack next to her bra.

"Too bad. I'd like to see them on."

"Another time." Her breath caught. That had slipped out so easily.

He gazed at her. "I look forward to it."

And just like that, their romp had expanded from one night of stolen bliss to additional encounters. "Anything else in the washer?"

"I think that's it." He peered inside the washer. "Nothing else."

"Good." She closed the door and switched on the dryer. "We can go back in—"

"Maybe not yet." He caught her around the waist and pulled her close. "I kind of like it here."

"I can tell." His cock pressed against her belly as he splayed his fingers over her bottom, caressing and arousing her. Didn't take much. "No soft surfaces, though."

"I just need a surface. Doesn't have to be soft." He tightened his grip and lifted her on top of the dryer.

The clothes tumbling beneath her added a subtle, erotic vibration. "You really are crazy."

"Crazy like a fox. Perfect height." He stepped in close, nudging her thighs apart. "Makes kissing you easy." Leaning in, he slipped his hand behind her neck and settled his mouth over hers.

Once he focused on seducing her with his tongue, she was a goner. Then he began lightly stroking her breasts, her hips and her thighs. She jettisoned her inhibitions and clutched his shoulders for balance. She was more than ready for him when he slipped two fingers into her slick channel.

He touched her with bold confidence, as if he knew...ah...exactly how to...mm. The slow, sensuous rhythm stole her breath. Breaking away from his kiss, she dragged in air.

"You like that?"

"*Yes.*"

"And this?" He shifted the angle, his fingertips making contact in a whole new way.

She gasped as her world began to splinter. She couldn't speak, couldn't say the words—*more, oh, please, more, just...*

He gave her more, ramping up the pace and increasing the pressure until her world spun out of control...until her body arched and the shock waves of her climax tore a cry of release from her throat.

Chest heaving, she gulped for air. "So good."

"Thought so." He trailed his damp fingers up her body and feathered a kiss over her mouth. "I have another idea."

"Better...let me...catch my breath."

"Absolutely." He tucked his hands under her bottom. "Just wrap your legs around my hips and your arms around my neck." He lifted her off the dryer. "I'll carry you."

"Where?"

"Since the electricity's still on—" He took her through the kitchen and kept going. "I'm in the mood for a shower."

Her pulse rate skyrocketed. "Need me to wash your back?"

"Yes, ma'am, I believe I do."

"My shower, then."

"Bigger?"

"Walk-in."

"Excellent." His long strides propelled them through the living room and down the hall. "Don't believe I've ever been in your bedroom." He stepped through the door and paused. "Hey, now. Nice big bed you have there, Miss Taryn." He gazed at it before returning his attention to her and lifting his eyebrows.

"Uh-huh."

"Is it the same one you had when you were—"

She shook her head. "Sold that. I bought this when I moved here."

"Good to know." He skirted the bed and carried her to the bathroom, heading straight toward the large tiled shower before putting her down right outside it. The maneuver was complicated by his impressively erect cock. He was breathing hard.

So was she. Heart thumping, she stepped in the shower, twisted the hot water knob and backed away, holding her hand under the spray to gauge when it was warm enough.

Air moved behind her, followed by a kiss on her shoulder. Sweeping her hair back, he placed more kisses along the curve of her neck as he slid a hand under her breast, cradling it in his palm, squeezing gently.

How quickly she caught fire when he touched her. "The water's...getting hot."

His soft chuckle, low and intimate, skittered over her nerve endings. "Me, too."

Easing away from him, she adjusted the temperature and moved aside. "See if that works for you."

Walking into the spray, he tipped back his head and closed his eyes. "Mm."

Stunning. Water lovingly caressed his sculpted body and his proud cock. His skin gleamed in the overhead light. She couldn't wait to get her hands on him. "Mind if I join you?"

Opening his eyes, he turned toward her with a smile. "If you don't, I'll be forced to solve this problem myself." He spread his arms wide. "I'm a desperate man."

"Can't have that." Moving into his open arms, her back to the spray, she cupped his face and pulled him down for an open-mouthed kiss.

With a groan, he gathered her close as water pelted his face, adding moisture to their erotic kiss and turning their hot bodies into slick instruments of pleasure. Sucking on his tongue, she slipped her hand over his taut abs and wrapped her fingers around his cock.

He trembled.

She lifted her mouth a fraction from his. "You okay?"

His voice was hoarse. "Never better."

"Oh, but you will be. Much better." Maintaining a firm hold on her ultimate prize, she licked her way down his heaving chest and over his quivering abs until she sank to her knees on the wet tile. Then she closed her mouth over the very tip of his warm cock.

He gasped.

Swirling her tongue lightly over the most sensitive spot of all, she tasted the salt of his impending climax, the one he'd held back each time he'd given her one. A groan rumbled in his broad chest.

He deserved this release, but he also deserved to have some fun before he got there. Circling the base of his shaft with her thumb and forefinger, she tightened her grip as she slowly took his full length into her mouth.

He made a sound low in his throat, almost a growl.

What a thrill to wrest such a primitive response from a man who always seemed in control of himself. Pulse racing, she gradually drew back, then took him in again. Warm water cascaded over her, sharpening all her senses.

His breathing roughened. She moved slightly faster this time, then faster yet, loosening her grip, then tightening it again. His thighs shook.

Then he spoke, his voice tight with strain. "Taryn. *Please.*"

She bore down, using her tongue, sucking hard. With a deafening roar that shook his whole body, he came. She accepted all he had to give.

When it was over, he drew her gently to her feet. He struggled for breath as his gaze locked with hers. "Thank you."

She smiled. "Good?"

"Incredible." Water dripped from his hair and gathered on his eyelashes. "We should probably turn off the shower."

"Probably."

"Just one more kiss." Cradling the back of her head, he angled his mouth over hers, sipping drops of water, licking them away. "Someday," he murmured, "we'll do this in the rain."

"But not naked."

"Don't rule it out." He ran his tongue over her lower lip.

"In the winter?"

"It won't always be winter." He combed her damp hair back from her face. "Before you know it, we'll have warm summer rains."

Summer? Had this episode just expanded to include summer? "And guests everywhere."

"Not everywhere." He smiled. "I'll bet we could find a secluded meadow."

Her chest tightened. She'd signed up for a romp. What he was describing sounded suspiciously like a romance.

She'd had one of those. It had clouded her thinking and blinded her to the problems lurking in the relationship.

She could deal with a romp. She might be able to handle an extended fling. As for romance, she wasn't in the market.

21

Pete was not only starving, he wanted to help cook dinner. Hanging around letting someone else handle the chores didn't sit well with him. Other than his specialty of French toast, he was no expert in the kitchen, but he was terrific at helping.

Taryn had spaghetti noodles and a jar of sauce she'd picked up at the Eagles Nest market. Interesting that she'd done that after proclaiming that she didn't normally keep standard dinner items on hand. Almost like she'd anticipated that they'd share another evening meal. In any case, he could help her put spaghetti together.

Deciding his clothes were dry enough, he pulled on his briefs, his jeans and his yoked shirt. His t-shirt was still damp around the neck, but he didn't absolutely have to put that on. Hanging out in the kitchen with Taryn should heat him up to the point he didn't need that extra layer.

She'd put on her PJs and slippers after the epic shower experience. She'd also used a blow dryer on her hair and had tried to talk him into blow-drying his. He'd refused, and she was still teasing him about it while they heated spaghetti sauce and cooked noodles.

"I don't get what's unmanly about aiming some warm air at your hair so it'll dry faster." She picked up a wooden spoon and stirred the noodles.

"It's not unmanly. I'm sure plenty of manly men do it. For me, though, it's unnecessary." The sauce was his responsibility and it was bubbling too much so he turned down the heat. "Most of the time I'm wearing a hat."

"Not tonight." She sauntered over and reached up to comb her fingers through his damp hair. "This could be completely dry if you hadn't stubbornly refused to take my—"

He grabbed her around the waist and pulled her close. "But now I have extra time to do this." He captured her mouth and settled in. In less than two seconds, she'd melted into that kiss and her tempting body had molded to his.

Lifting his head, he gazed into her heavy-lidded eyes. "Or maybe I should blow-dry my hair."

"Shut up and kiss me."

He grinned. "Okay, since I have the time." He lowered his head and the kitchen lights flickered. "Uh-oh."

"Power going out?"

"Maybe not. It might only be—" The house went dark, the fridge clicked off and so did the stove. Warm air no longer blew through the heater vents. A deep silence reigned. "It could come back on. Sometimes it's only a temporary glitch."

"Sure is dark. And quiet. I've been in blackouts before, but I was in the city. You still had cars going by with their lights on, and some buildings had a generator. You're probably used to this total darkness."

"Kind of." Still startling, though.

"We should pull the battery-operated lanterns and the candles out of the storeroom." She laughed. "If only we could see."

"My phone's on the kitchen table. I'll get it." He found the table but stubbed his bare toe on the leg of a chair. "Damn."

"What's wrong?"

"Nothing." He patted the surface of the table until he located his phone.

"Don't tell me *nothing*. I heard a thump and then you swore."

"Stubbed my toe on the leg of a kitchen chair. I'm fine." He turned on his flashlight app and handed her his phone.

She swept the beam toward his feet. "I don't see blood. Guess I can believe you." Walking into the storeroom, she focused the light on the shelves, took down a lantern and switched it on. "Wow, that's bright."

He leaned in the doorway. "There's probably a way to dim it."

"Yeah, but more is better, right?"

"Guess so, at least for getting dinner ready. I see you bought candles in glass jars. Good move. Much safer that way."

"But we don't need to bother with them."

"Why not?" He pushed away from the doorframe as she walked out and gave him the phone.

"Don't need 'em. The lantern will do the trick."

Weren't women supposed to love candlelight? "It will, but would you mind if I lit a couple of those candles and put them in the living room?"

She gave him a funny look. "Um, sure. Go ahead." She held the lantern near the doorway.

Walking in, he took down two of the candle jars. Scented with cinnamon and clove, too. He came back out and closed the storage room door. "Might as well have a little atmosphere with our power outage. I'll go light these and build up the fire."

"Hey, that's right. The fire is our only source of heat."

Yes, it was, and she'd had to point it out to him. He'd been more focused on creating ambiance for a romantic interlude than preparing for a night without central heating. Time to get his head in the game. "Come on back to your bedroom with me."

Her eyes widened.

"Not for that, unfortunately. We need to haul bedding into the living room and I don't know which blankets you—"

"Ah. I get it. Come on." She left the kitchen, lantern held high to light their way.

He left the candles on an end table as he passed by. "I'll bring in more wood from the laundry room so we'll have a supply handy.

Closing off all the other rooms will help contain the heat."

"And drawing the living room curtains. They're still open." She walked into the bedroom and set the lantern on her dresser. "What's the longest you've ever gone without electricity?"

"About fifteen minutes."

"*Whaaat?*" She spun to face him.

"We had a generator at the Lazy S the whole time I lived there. Evidently my mother insisted on it because there were babies in the house."

"And here I thought you were a veteran of the power outage wars."

"I am. We always operated as if we might get completely cut off. Dad kept the generator maintained, but it was a machine. Machines malfunction. We were stocked with battery-operated lanterns, candles and plenty of firewood."

"Just like me."

"We'll be fine. We have wood, blankets—"

"And each other."

"True." His brain took a hike down the sensuality trail. Couldn't avoid that tantalizing route, especially when she was showing him the way.

"Everyone knows getting naked and hugging each other keeps you from freezing to death."

"Uh-huh." Fire licked his privates and her bed was steps away. He sucked in air. "Let's get those blankets."

* * *

Pete had done everything he could think of to prepare for hours without electricity. He'd brought in more wood from the laundry room and filled the bathtub with water. Their dinner dishes had been cleared but left unwashed. Blankets were piled on the end of the couch, available for when they decided to make up their bed on the floor in front of the fireplace. Pillows were stacked on both easy chairs.

He'd moved the coffee table after dinner but hadn't suggested creating their bed yet. Neither had she. Instead he'd cuddled up with her on the other half of the couch. They weren't making out, either, although the possibility hovered in the background.

For the time being, they'd settled in to watch the fire and just...talk. He'd convinced her that they didn't need the lantern since they had firelight and the glow from the spice-scented candles.

Truth be told, he couldn't come up with anything more he required at this moment. Gazing into the flames and discussing plans for Crimson Clouds with Taryn snuggled in the crook of his arm was his version of paradise.

Well, some of those little raincoats would be nice, but other than that, he couldn't be any happier. Desire simmered under the surface, bubbling up whenever she shifted slightly in his arms and her scent teased him. Or when she looked up at him, laughter in her eyes, and the laughter gradually transformed to heat.

He held off kissing her because once he did, their clothes would come off and this moment would become something else entirely. He wanted that, too, but this...this was special.

It wasn't like they were ignoring the sensuality linking them. As she broached the subject of expanding their herd of horses, she casually rested her hand on his thigh. Her touch penetrated the denim, traveled to his groin, spread warmth, but not so much that he had to take action.

As he laid out his thoughts on their next horse-buying venture, he lazily traced the curve of her ear with one finger.

"I would love an appaloosa." Her voice took on a low, intimate quality. "So beautiful and so interesting to look at."

"Expensive."

"I know." She drew a figure-eight pattern on his thigh. "I can wait. See how the summer goes."

He toyed with a lock of her hair, brushing it against her cheek. "Maybe we'll find a smokin' deal."

"That would be nice." She sounded a little breathless. "Speaking of smoke, the—"

"Fire needs tending." He levered himself off the couch. His jeans pinched as he crouched on the hearth. Conversation time might be over.

He rearranged the logs and added two more. Standing, he replaced the screen, turned and sucked in a breath. She lay naked on the couch, propped against the mound of blankets.

Her seductive smile added to the pressure building behind his fly. Swinging her feet to the floor, she rose, grabbed a pillow from the closest easy chair and tossed it his way. "Ready to check out the scientific evidence on naked bodies and warmth?"

22

Taryn couldn't vouch for the purity of her research methods, but her naked body writhing against Pete's generated a hell of a lot of heat. He made her come again and she returned the favor. After their energetic lovemaking, she had no need for a comforter. And talk about relaxed. Her eyes drifted closed.

Pete lay on his back beside her, his head on a fluffy pillow, his hand entwined with hers as his breathing slowed. "Epic."

"Yep."

"Not that we need it, but I'd better add a couple of logs to the fire. Don't want it to go out." Giving her hand a squeeze, he left their cozy nest.

Rolling to her side, she struggled to keep her eyes open because Pete naked in front of the fire was a fabulous visual.

He returned and stretched out facing her. "Can't speak for you, but I'm lovin' this blizzard."

"Me, too." She covered a yawn. "But I just realized that if we fall asleep, there will be nobody to tend the fire."

"Don't worry." He reached over and stroked her cheek. "I'll keep it going."

"How? I'm getting sleepy, and you've been awake as many hours as I have. You also chopped all that wood."

He grinned. "And made all that love."

"Exactly. You won't be able to stay awake."

"You're right. I won't. But I'll set my internal alarm." Leaning closer, he kissed her gently. "Go to sleep. I'll keep watch."

She stifled another yawn. "Doesn't seem fair."

"Sure it is. I chose to stay so I could keep you safe. And warm."

She gave up the effort to keep her eyes open. "Good job on that."

He chuckled. "Thanks. Want the comforter over you?"

"Not yet. Still...very...warm."

"Okay." He kissed her again.

Five minutes later, or so it seemed, she woke up with a start. Pete had covered them with the comforter and another blanket. He was asleep, his breathing slow and even, his cheeks and chin darkened with stubble. Propping herself on one arm, she looked beyond him to the fire, which was crackling merrily.

The log rack was nearly empty. She'd been asleep for hours and Pete, true to his word, had kept the fire going. He must have been awake only minutes ago and she certainly didn't want to disturb him, now.

Lying down again, she took a deep breath and looked up at the beamed ceiling above her. She admired Pete's heroics, but his dedication unsettled her a bit. There was nothing casual about his—

Wait. She could see the beams above her. And the couch beside her. Pale gray light came through a break in the drapes covering the picture window. The wind no longer howled and battered the house. It was morning. The blizzard was over.

Moving carefully, she eased out from under the covers and stood. Her pajamas were where she'd left them on the couch, along with her slippers. She put everything on and walked toward the window.

The temperature dropped with every step away from the fireplace but she kept going, pulled by curiosity. No telling how it would look outside. Yikes. It was *freezing* over by the window.

Shivering, she parted the curtains and peered out. Couldn't see a thing through a layer of crackled ice covering the window. Pretty with light shining through it. She'd appreciate nature's handiwork more if her teeth would stop chattering.

At least snow wasn't blocking the window, which meant she wouldn't open the door and find a wall of snow. She wouldn't have to shovel it into her galvanized tub and carry it to the bathtub.

Except that wouldn't have worked because the bathtub was full of water. Maybe Pete had intended to put the snow, if they had to shovel it, in her shower, instead. She had faith that he'd had a system in place. The guy had managed to keep the fire going between catnaps.

Rustling from the vicinity of their makeshift bed alerted her that he was awake. She turned away from the window.

"Morning." He flashed her a smile as he stepped into his knit briefs and pulled them up. If the company that made them could see how he looked in their product, they'd sign him to a modeling contract in a heartbeat.

"Morning. It's stopped."

"I know. Realized that when I woke up to take care of the fire." He put on his jeans and zipped them.

Last night he'd had quite a struggle unzipping them. Her pose on the couch had created an instant reaction. But that was last night, when they'd been snowbound. If the blizzard was gone, they could dig themselves out, rejoin the rest of the world. Maybe that was a good thing.

"Still no power, though." He picked up his shirt. "We'll have to—ha! There it is!" All the lights came on—the lamps in the living room, the multicolored strands on the Christmas tree and the overhead light in the kitchen. The heat kicked into gear, too, sending warm air pouring from the vents. He fastened the snaps of his shirt. "The crisis is over."

"Didn't feel like one."

"Sure didn't. More like a...I'm not sure what to call it."

"Forbidden fantasy?"

"I'll go with fantasy." He tucked his shirt into his jeans. "But I hope it wasn't forbidden." He paused to glance at her. "That sounds too much like a one-time thing."

She walked in his direction, but chose to keep the couch between them. "It's not, but—"

"Thank God. Because I'm not ready to pretend this never happened. I'm willing to have you set the rules, but I'll say this right up front—I want to spend the night with you again. And next time I'll be better prepared."

His bold statement heated her blood. She almost said *tonight*, but caught herself. She'd already lost perspective thanks to his wonderful lovemaking and his heroic behavior. She needed to regroup. "How about Saturday night, after the talent show?"

His frown came and went quickly. He followed it with a smile. "That would be great." He hesitated. "Are you okay with me letting my dad know I'll be gone that night? It's not like he monitors my life, but I live there, and Clifford is my responsibility, not his."

"Absolutely let your dad know. He's a perceptive man. He's likely already guessed something's going on between us."

"I'm sure of it. Doesn't seem worried about it, either. Unlike my uncle, who—" He stopped abruptly.

"What about your uncle?"

"Not important. Hey, I'll bet those horses are ready for breakfast. I'll head down there and feed them while you get dressed."

"Not on your life. I'm going with you. I'm dying to see what my ranch looks like buried in snow." She pointed a finger at him. "Wait for me."

He laughed. "Yes, ma'am. I'll bank the fire if we're both heading out. And start some coffee for when we get back, if you want me to."

"That would be awesome." She hurried down the hall to her bedroom, where the blanket and comforter were stripped off. She made a quick trip to the bathroom and caught sight of herself in the mirror. Her hair looked as if she'd stepped into a wind tunnel, and in a way, she had. Pete's style of loving would blow any woman's hair back.

After dressing quickly in the warmest clothes she owned, she dug into the back reaches of her closet and came up with her Wellingtons. They weren't Western wear, but they would work great in snow drifts. Last of all she tugged on a knit hat—not the one her mother had made, but a store-bought version. She wouldn't win a beauty contest in this getup, but she might stay warm.

When she walked into the living room, Pete grinned. "I love that outfit on you."

"Then you're seriously whacked. There's nothing remotely sexy about what I'm wearing."

"True."

"So why do you love it?"

"Because you're letting me see the real Taryn Maroney, the one who doesn't give a damn what she looks like. She just wants to be warm and cozy."

"That's a fact." She went over to the door and grabbed her parka from the hook on the wall. "And you're the only one here to see me. For seven months, you've arrived at dawn and found me in old clothes and no makeup. There are no illusions for me to destroy."

"I'm not interested in illusions." He reached for her. "Hang on a second."

"What?"

"Before you disappear into your parka, I have something to say." He drew her closer.

She gazed up at him. Those warm gray eyes gave her heart palpitations. "What's that?"

"Last night was amazing."

"No argument there."

"If that was the one and only time I ever had with you, I'd still count myself a lucky bastard."

"Thank you."

"But I'm also a greedy bastard. That's why I announced I wanted to spend the night again. I didn't give you much chance to say no."

"I want to spend another night with you, too. I just need...time to catch my breath."

"I understand." He hesitated. "But like I said, I'm greedy. I asked for another night, but—"

She gently placed her finger against his lips. Then she traced the outline of his mouth. "Let's talk about it on Saturday."

He let out a breath. "We can do that." He brushed a thumb over her lower lip. "I would love to kiss you right now, except I seem to have grown a beard during the night."

"I noticed. I've never seen you like that."

"Hope it doesn't scare you off."

"I kind of like it."

"Yeah?"

"Yeah." Standing on tiptoe, she gave him a quick kiss, stepped back and shoved her arms into the sleeves of her parka. "Time to feed those critters and see what Mother Nature has done to this place." She zipped her parka, dug out her gloves and put them on.

"Yes, ma'am." He put on his hat and gloves.

"Can't wait." After unlocking the door, she turned the knob and pulled. Nothing happened. She took off her gloves, braced her feet and gave it all she had. Didn't budge. "It's like it's welded shut!"

"Want me to try?"

She blew out a breath. "What if you weren't here? What if I couldn't get out my own front door?"

"You'd have to figure it out."

"That's right." She paused. "Be right back."

When she returned with her hair dryer, Pete laughed. "Excellent."

"This is going to work." She plugged it into a nearby outlet and aimed the hot air along the edge of the door. "I realize that if the power hadn't come on, I'd have to think of something else, like heating water over the fire and using steam."

"Regardless, you have the right idea."

She shut off the dryer. "Maybe that's enough." After unplugging it, she put on her gloves. "Here goes." The door stuck at first, but then with a loud crack, it opened. She stumbled but kept her balance. "Ta-da!"

"Great job. I'll bring the shovels."

"Damn, it's cold out here!" She didn't pause to look at the wintry scene. They had to get out and close that door.

She stepped quickly over a two-foot drift that had piled against the door and her boots sank through a layer of snow on the porch. Pete came out behind her with the shovels. She turned around to take one so he could grab the knob and close the door.

There. Facing forward, she gasped, sucking in frigid air that made her chest hurt. Snow obscured everything—including the steps and the decorative fence.

Only the curve of the arch and the top of the spruce trees protruded from the thick white blanket. Beyond the yard, drifts had stacked against the barn doors. The top rail of the corral seemed to rest on a cushion of snow and all the posts wore white puffy hats.

Pete wrapped his arm around her shoulders. "What do you think?"

"It's beautiful, absolutely beautiful. And we have a whole lot of shoveling to do."

23

      Taryn wielded a snow shovel with enthusiasm, which came as no surprise to Pete. Hard physical work had never intimidated her. The trick was getting her to pace herself. Challenged with this much snow removal, she was liable to shovel to the point where she would be painfully sore in the morning.

      Once the horses were fed and the stalls mucked out, he talked her into taking time out for breakfast. They left their boots, coats and hats by the door and he started cooking while she changed out of her wet clothes. His jeans were a little damp, but not bad. He'd had more practice at staying dry while shoveling.

      Over bacon, eggs, toast and coffee, she brought up the subject of her road, which was currently impassable. "I can't believe I didn't plan for this." She finished her coffee and got up to bring the pot over. "Want more?"

      "Yes, please." More of everything. The blizzard had been a challenge, but he was sad it was over. Didn't want to wait until Saturday night to hold her again. Her call, though.

"Anyway, I completely spaced the road situation. Did you think of it? That I wouldn't be prepared if I got snowed in?"

"I knew you didn't have equipment to plow the road, but I wasn't worried about it."

"Why not? Surely the town won't come out and plow all these rural roads."

"They don't have the resources, but if I know my dad, he's in road-plowing mode even as we speak. That man loves driving a tractor. Once he's finished his road and Kendra's, he'll be over to take care of yours."

"Well, that's very nice of him, but now that I've experienced a blizzard up close and personal, I want a tractor, too."

He grinned. "Is that right?"

"Why not? That utility vehicle you mentioned the other day might handle minor snow removal but not something like this. Besides, a tractor would be fun. A big ol' green machine. What's the brand everybody talks about?"

"John Deere."

"That's it. I want to learn to drive a John Deere."

"Then I'd be happy to teach you. I'm partial to tractors, myself."

"Are you saying you'd want to drive it?"

"Heck, yeah. Dad and I used to toss a coin to see which one of us got to plow the road after a heavy snowstorm."

"Sounds like a love of tractors runs in your family."

"Yep. My dad says owning a ranch is mostly a good excuse to buy a tractor."

"I wish I'd figured that out sooner, but I totally agree with him. What's the point in living in the boonies unless you get to play with all the toys?"

"Good point." Taryn had just shot past his expectations...again. "After Christmas we'll go tractor shopping, see who'll give us a deal."

"Good. I'm excited."

"Me, too. I—" His phone chimed. "That's probably my dad, alerting us that he's—nope, my uncle. Excuse me a minute." He put the phone to his ear. "Hey, Uncle Brendan."

"G'day, mate." His Crocodile Dundee accent was especially thick this morning. "Just giving you a heads-up that I'm about to start motatin' your way with the tractor."

"Dad's letting you plow?"

His uncle laughed. "Yea, yea. Aced the coin toss."

"I see."

"I'm particularly happy about that because I'm hankerin' to meet your lady."

"That's not, um, the designation I'd use." Should have taken the call in the living room.

"It didn't work out last night? Now that's shame."

"A shame? I thought you were..." He trailed off. Couldn't go into it.

"Worried? Nah. Quinn convinced me your situation is nothing like mine was. Consequently, I'm pullin' for you. Chances are you weren't fully prepared, though. That can be a problem."

"Everything's fine."

"I sense a complication."

"Not really."

"She's right there, isn't she?"

"Yes."

"Ah. Sorry, mate. Anyway, forget what I said before. Enjoy yourself."

Pete couldn't help smiling at that. "Thanks. I will."

"Good on ya. We need more hanky-panky in this world. See you soon."

"Appreciate it, Uncle Brendan." He disconnected the call. "He won the coin toss. He's coming instead of my dad."

"Wonderful! Then I'll get to meet him." She glanced at him, a gleam in her eyes. "He was asking about last night, wasn't he?"

"He was." He sighed. "I'm afraid we'll be a topic of conversation for the next few days, especially because everyone will be together so much. I don't know how to avoid the attention focused on us, and I hope—"

"Pete, I don't mind." She reached over and squeezed his arm. "They all love you. Naturally they'll wonder about this new development. Shoot, *I'm* wondering about it."

Grasping her hand, he brought it to his lips. "I'll never hurt you. I can promise you that."

She drew in a shaky breath. "I can't make you any promises."

"I'm not asking for any. I never expected to be your lover. I thought that was a non-starter. But here we are. Every minute with you is a bonus."

Warmth flickered in her eyes. "Same here."

"You are looking so kissable right now, and me with porcupine face."

"Want to borrow my razor?"

"Thanks, but I don't dare start kissing you when Uncle Brendan's on his way." He pushed back his chair. "Let's clean up these dishes."

"Alrighty."

He stacked the plates and carried them over to the counter. "I'll bring my shaving kit Saturday night, though. I don't like not being able to kiss you."

"Might as well bring a change of clothes, too." She brought over the mugs and the coffee carafe.

"Thought I would." He started loading the dishwasher. "Wouldn't mind making up a bed in front of the fireplace again, too. After having sex on a blanket with a fire crackling nearby, a bed seems kind of boring." He put a mug in the top rack and glanced at her. "Speaking of that, are the blankets and pillows still in the living room?"

"Guess so. I didn't—" Her eyes widened. "Good grief. We need to get them out of there before your uncle arrives." She bolted from the room.

He followed quickly behind. It was one thing for his uncle to know something had gone on here. He didn't need to view the evidence.

"Don't try folding anything." She grabbed several pillows. "Just bundle it up and bring it back to my bedroom." She raced down the hall in her sock feet.

"Got it." Arms full of bedding, he lengthened his stride. They likely had enough time. Then again, if his uncle drove a tractor the way he did everything, no holds barred, he could already be barreling down Taryn's road with snow flying every which way.

"Just dump that on my bed."

He dropped the comforter and blankets on the mattress.

She glanced at him. "What's left?"

"I'm pretty sure I got it all, but let's go look."

She started back down the hall. "I'm glad you remembered. I suppose it's silly, since he knows we messed around."

"It's not silly." He walked behind her down the narrow hallway. "This is our business. Nobody else needs to know the details."

She looked over her shoulder. "Thanks for that. I've discovered moving to a small town means you're living in a fish bowl, but some things..."

"That's my point. People can imagine all they want, but I'm not giving them any help in that department. If we decide to get out some velvet handcuffs and a can of whipped cream, they'll never hear it from me."

She stopped so fast he had to backpedal to keep from running into her. She spun around. "What did you say?"

"I don't know. Spewing some sort of nonsense. Why?"

"Velvet handcuffs and whipped cream? Are you serious?"

"Not really." He hesitated. "Unless you are."

Her eyes sparkled with mischief. "What if I am?"

"Then I guess I'd..." She could be joking, but despite that, lust took over his brain, short-circuiting logic. "I'd pick up some whipped cream for Saturday night. The velvet handcuffs might require a trip to Bozeman, and even so, I'm not sure I could find—"

"You're adorable."

He smiled. "Not a primo compliment, FYI. People say that about babies and puppies. Kittens sometimes, or stuffed animals."

"I guess adorable's the wrong word if you're willing to drive twenty-six miles on icy roads to buy velvet handcuffs. Never mind adorable. I'm going with crazy."

"I'd do it for you."

"Crazy. Insane, bonkers. Take your pick. Fortunately, I'm not into velvet handcuffs."

"Whipped cream?"

"Goes great on strawberry shortcake and pumpkin pie."

"How about on my—" A fist thumped twice on the front door.

"Your uncle's here. We didn't make a final sweep."

"You get the door. I'll make the sweep."

More thumping on the door. "Pete! You in there, mate?"

She gazed at him. "You didn't finish your sentence. Whipped cream on your what?"

He laughed. "Tongue."

"Liar." She started for the door.

24

Taryn fell madly in love with Brendan Sawyer. He was so like her parents, determined to take life in big gulps, easy to talk to and tease. As she sat with him and Pete drinking coffee and eating the last of the chocolate fudge cookies, she traded jokes with him as if she'd known him for years.

She pushed the cookie package in his direction with a singsong *chocolate is your friend.*

He laughed and took another one, giving her a smile and a thank you.

"Tell me, Brendan. How is it that you haven't given your heart to some lovely Australian woman?"

"There's the rub, you see. They're lovely and I'm not. I never could bridge that gap. Whereas my handsome nephew, here—" He gestured toward Pete. "He has a much easier time of it."

Pete chuckled and shook his head. "Not true."

His uncle rolled his eyes. "You're not supposed to contradict me, mate."

"Why not?"

"I'm tryin' to make you look like a studly fellow in the eyes of this amazin' young woman."

"Never easy."

"Well, here's a dandy trick that works every time. Go fire up that tractor and clear some space in the pasture so she can turn out her horses." Brendan glanced at her. "That'd impress the heck out of you, right?"

"Absolutely. Especially if it includes my first lesson in driving one."

Brendan's eyebrows lifted. "Didn't know you had an interest."

"After the holidays, Pete and I are going tractor shopping."

"Well, now." Brendan looked over at his nephew. "Seems like a tractor lesson will win you even more points."

"Does seem that way."

"Then let's do it." He stood. "While you two play with Quinn's tractor, I'll head into the barn and get acquainted with your horses. Then I'll take the tractor and go home. Wouldn't want to wear out my welcome."

Taryn gave him a smile. "Don't see that happening."

An hour later, the horses frolicked in the cleared section of the pasture and Taryn had a new appreciation for the intricacies of driving a tractor. She stood beside the barn with Pete and waved goodbye as Brendan climbed behind the wheel, put it in gear and rumbled out of the yard.

"And that's my Uncle Brendan."

"He's terrific."

"He thinks the same of you."

"He said that?"

"Didn't have to. I could tell by his expression." He turned to face her. "So how'd you like the tractor? Still want one?"

"More than ever. There's so much we can do with it. Clearly I'll need practice before I'm comfortable with the whole gear thing, though. For some reason, I thought it would be like driving a car."

"More complicated than that."

"No kidding, but I'm determined to master it." She grinned. "Your uncle was right, though. You look studly maneuvering that tractor."

"Even more reason to buy one. I had no idea sitting up on a tractor would improve my image."

"It's not just sitting up there. Now that I know the skill involved, it's a pleasure watching you drive it like it's second nature."

"Does it get you hot?"

"Maybe."

He gazed at her. "Want to do anything about that?"

"I'm tempted, but...no." She rested her gloved hands on his chest. "I was serious about needing some time to process all this. I can handle feeding tonight."

Smiling, he drew her close. "I get the feeling it's time to make my exit."

She nodded. "Much as I hate to see you go. But I know myself. This has been a big change for both of us. I can't speak for you, but—"

"I'd call it a welcome change, but I get your point. I'll take off, give you some space."

"Thanks." Relief loosened the slight tension in her shoulders. "You know what? Let me handle feeding in the morning, too. You haven't taken a day off this week."

He frowned. "No big deal. We've had unusual circumstances. I can certainly—"

"But it's the holidays. For all I know you have Christmas shopping to do."

"Hm. Come to think of it…"

"Then it's settled. You can pick me up after lunch tomorrow so we can watch Josh sit on Santa's lap. I can't wait to see how that turns out."

"Me, either. We'll have to make a quick trip back here to feed before the talent show."

"That won't take long. What a fun day it'll be."

"Followed by a fun night." He pulled her hips against his.

"Mm." She soaked up the passion in his gaze as delicious heat flowed between them. "That'll be nice."

"Tell me about it. We have about a million layers between us and I can still feel you getting hot."

"And I can feel your—"

"Yep, and that's why I'm going to skedaddle before that situation intensifies." Leaning down, he dropped a soft kiss on her mouth. "I'll check with Gage and let you know when they're planning to take Josh over there."

"Perfect."

"See you then." Touching two fingers to the brim of his hat, he walked to his truck. It didn't want to start right away but he eventually got it running. He tooted his horn as he passed by and she waved.

Then she pressed her hand against the hollow ache in her chest as his truck turned onto the newly plowed road. He wasn't even out of sight and she missed him. Made sense. He'd literally been her lifeline for the past twenty-four hours.

A horse nickered and she turned toward the pasture, grateful for the distraction. Honey Butter stood about ten feet from the gate. He was watching her.

"Are you looking for some attention, big guy?" Walking over to the gate, she opened it, slipped inside and closed it behind her.

The palomino came over and nuzzled her pocket.

"No treats in there this time." She scratched his neck and combed her fingers through his cream-colored mane. "Good thing you had your close-up two days ago, buddy. You're looking a little rough around the edges."

The other five, clearly wondering if they were missing something, wandered toward her. Yesterday she and Pete had scraped off most of the melted snow, but they hadn't groomed any of them. They could use it.

"Okay, my friends. I'm taking you all into the barn and giving you a beauty treatment. Taryn's salon is now open for business."

Twenty minutes later, they were in their respective stalls munching a small helping of oats. She worked her way down the line with the grooming tote, brushing their thick winter coats, untangling manes and tails, complimenting them on their good looks.

She ended with Honey Butter. "You looked good in that video, buddy, with Pete riding you bareback." Her hand stilled as she treated herself to a replay of that moment.

With a sigh, she resumed her vigorous brushing. "So here's the thing. After making a mistake and marrying the wrong guy, I'm not interested in getting involved with anyone right now. But I got caught up in the moment and kissed Pete when we were up in the bucket."

The palomino snorted.

"Look, that's my excuse and I'm sticking to it. Wasn't thinking ahead. Wasn't thinking at all. Then we had the blizzard and...things have escalated."

Across the way, Fifty Shades whinnied.

She laughed. "Yep, you said it! Like a gallop across the meadow that's somewhat out of control." She went around to Honey Butter's other side, finished brushing him, and picked up a smaller brush for his mane. "Anyway, I needed a timeout, so I sent him home until tomorrow. I think it's the right thing for both of us to take a break.

Honey Butter nodded his head.

"Thank you! It *is* a good plan. Twenty-four hours will give us both a chance to cool off and gain some perspective. Because this might work if we just don't get too emotionally involved."

Junior's nicker from the next stall sounded like laughter. Then Spike made the same comment.

"Okay, you guys. Laugh if you want, but I say it's possible. A friends-with-benefits sort of arrangement. Casual but fun. That's what I'm going for." She stood in front of the palomino and brushed his forelock. "Wish me luck."

Honey Butter gently bumped his nose against her chest.

"Thanks, sweetie." She gave him a kiss and put away the brush. "Appreciate the support."

25

Good thing Taryn had mentioned Christmas shopping. He'd already shopped for the rest of his family. The gifts were wrapped and hidden in his closet at home. That left him free to spend the afternoon coming up with ideas for Taryn.

It turned out he had several and he didn't want to narrow the list so he got everything. He couldn't expect her to open all of them on Christmas at Wild Creek Ranch, though. That would shine too bright a spotlight on their new relationship. One present was enough for the family gathering. The rest he'd take over Saturday night as a surprise.

And why not a bottle of champagne from the Eagles Nest Market for their special night together? He could stick it in an insulated cooler in the back of his truck, both to disguise it and make sure it didn't freeze. When Otto, the market's owner, spotted him buying the champagne, he convinced him to get a small poinsettia in a decorative pot. That also could go in the cooler along with the Christmas cookies he'd picked up at Pie in the Sky.

The following afternoon he put the cooler in the bed of his truck along with the box of gifts. Then he threw a tarp over everything and used a few rocks to keep it in place.

He parked in front of the walkway. She'd shoveled that since he was here and cleaned off the porch steps, too. The twenty-four hours he'd been gone seemed much longer. Leaving the motor running and the heater on, he went up the steps and across the porch.

She opened the door before he could knock. "Hey, there." Instead of her parka, she wore a white winter coat he'd never seen. Her dark green scarf looped around her neck matched her jeans, which looked new. Her polished black boots were unfamiliar, too, and she was wearing makeup.

"Whoa. You look amazing."

"Thanks." She stepped out and closed the door. "I'll switch to my parka when we feed, but today feels like dress-up time."

"It does. Dusted off my best hat for the occasion. Guess I shouldn't kiss you, though."

"Better not. The lipstick's supposed to be kiss-proof but when I blotted it, some came off. I doubt you want to be wearing lipstick when we walk into Pills and Pop."

"I'd rather not." He took off his hat. "I'll just have to kiss you somewhere else." Leaning down, he drew her wool scarf aside and pressed his mouth against her warm throat. Her pulse fluttered beneath his lips and he nipped her soft skin. Gently. He didn't want to leave a mark.

She sucked in a breath. "That's...very..."

"Hope so." He lifted his head and gazed into her eyes. "Good to see you again." He resisted the urge to repeat the kiss. "We should get going." Putting on his hat, he tugged on the brim. "Don't want to miss Josh's big moment." He took her hand and started back down the walkway. "You've shoveled a lot of snow since I was here."

"Yep. It's almost as good as mucking out stalls for organizing my thoughts."

"All organized, now?" He helped her into the truck.

"Uh, huh."

"Glad to hear it." He hurried around to the driver's side and climbed in. Once they were headed down her road, he glanced over at her. "Want to share any of those neatly organized thoughts?"

"Maybe later. In front of the fire."

He sucked in a breath. "O-*kay*. Now let's change the subject so I don't drive into a ditch."

She laughed. "Fair enough. This is the first time I've been on this road since your uncle bladed it. Excellent job."

"He'll love hearing you say that."

"I'll get a chance, right? He'll be at Wild Creek Ranch for Christmas Eve and Christmas Day?"

"He wouldn't miss it. He's a party guy. He'll be at Pills and Pop for Josh's big moment with Santa, too. He said it's his duty now that he's Great-Uncle Brendan. He takes that seriously."

"Not as seriously as your dad takes being Grandpa Quinn, I'll bet."

"You have no idea." He turned onto the main road leading to town. "If he could have gotten away with it, he would have hired an entire film crew for this Santa gig."

"Did he at least hire Caitlin?"

"Yes. Gage and Emma were fine with that."

"Then she'll be there. I look forward to seeing her. She did such a terrific job on Wednesday that it'll be great to tell her so in person."

"My dad and Kendra are very happy with her work. Near as I can tell, she's become the official McGavin/Sawyer family photographer."

"Then she may be able to afford an assistant sooner than she thought."

"She wants one?"

"Partly to help her schlep her stuff around. Then she can concentrate on the job and the client."

"Then, yeah, I predict she'll be able to hire somebody soon. This combined family is very good at creating photo ops." Traffic grew heavier as he neared the outskirts of town, heavy being a relative term when it came to Eagles Nest. Three vehicles lined up on either side of the town's only stoplight qualified as a traffic jam. Four was considered freeway-style gridlock.

Taryn peered out the windshield. "I've never seen it like this."

"Neither have I, but it's the Saturday before Christmas."

"Last chance to tell Santa what you want for Christmas."

"What do you want?" He tossed it out as a joke, but discovered he was extremely interested in her answer.

"That's easy. A full roster of guests for the summer season. And a tractor. And if Santa's really feeling generous, a beautiful appaloosa."

"That's it?"

"Oh, wait. I want to hear the horses talk on Christmas Eve. What do you want?"

"A parking space."

"Oh, come on, you have to think bigger than that."

"Okay. I want my own house. And a barn." He'd never said that to anyone. Had barely admitted it to himself. For some reason it popped out now as he scanned the street in vain looking for something to open up.

"You do? I thought you were perfectly happy at your dad's."

"I am happy there. I wouldn't say I'm *perfectly* happy. In the back of my mind, I've been thinking that it would be nice to have my own place. I think it's time."

"Where would it be?"

"Around here, naturally. I—ha! Backup lights. That spot is *mine*."

"Woo-hoo!"

"And it's only two doors down from Pills and Pop." He put on his turn signal, waited for the other vehicle to back out, and pulled in.

"So you want a house and barn for Christmas?"

"Maybe not for Christmas, exactly, but soon. I want furniture that belongs to me. My own fireplace." He shut off the motor and flashed her a smile. "Let's go see Santa."

Opening his door, he hopped down and went around to open hers. "I can't believe this entire crowd is going to watch Josh sit on Santa's lap, but I still predict Pills and Pop will be standing room only."

"I can take it." She put her hand in his and climbed down. "As a teenager I stood for hours in a sea of people at music concerts."

"Me, too."

"Rock?"

"Country." He kept hold of her hand as they stepped up on the sidewalk and started toward the drugstore.

"I should have known. You were humming *I Like It, I Love It* in the shower night before last."

"How did you hear that all the way in the laundry room?"

"Um, I might not have left right away."

"Why not?"

"That was a sexy move, handing your clothes out through the door."

"What was I supposed to do? Throw them at you?"

"You did the right thing. I just wasn't prepared to see your bare arm come out. And then I realized it was connected to the rest of you."

He started laughing. "I should hope to howdy. Otherwise we're living in a horror flick."

"You know what I mean. I was picturing you naked, and thinking about that temporarily nailed me to the floor."

"Oh." He grinned. "Thanks for telling me. I can live on that for weeks."

<u>26</u>

So Pete wanted a place of his own. Not surprising, now that he wasn't in business with his dad anymore. Maybe he'd buy something closer to Crimson Clouds, so he'd have an easier commute.

Having him nearby would terrific, but it wasn't like he'd hired a real estate agent and was looking at property. They'd had an idle conversation about what they'd like for Christmas and she'd learned something new about Pete.

"Hey, you two!" Caitlin approached the drugstore from the other direction. "I'm so glad I caught you. Quinn just texted me and said it's a madhouse in there, but I wanted to share something cool with you." She glanced at their linked hands and smiled but didn't comment.

Taryn caught the glance. She hadn't thought about the significance of holding hands with Pete in public. In Eagles Nest it was probably an announcement of sorts. Oh, well.

"What's your news?" Caitlin's eyes sparkled as if she expected it to be something personal and romantic.

"I put your video up along with info for next year's Christmas special. It looks awesome, too."

"That's great! I'm amazed you got that done in the middle of a blizzard."

"Just made it before we lost power. It's so lucky you came out when you did."

"I thought of that, too. Anyway, my news is that the clip I put on my site of Pete helping Josh play the kazoo has gone viral."

Pete shoved back his hat. "You're kidding."

"Nope. It's showing up all over the place. People are turning it into memes with captions like *Party On*. The exposure should be great for my business, so I wanted to thank you."

"I'm glad it's doing good things for you."

Taryn pulled out her phone. "I'm going to look for it."

"Just search *Cowboy with baby playing kazoo.*"

"Got it! So cute. This one's titled *Make a Joyful Noise.* I love it." She glanced up at Pete. "You're famous."

"For about fifteen minutes. Tomorrow it'll be a video of a duck wearing a bikini."

"Sadly, that's true." Caitlin glanced at the time on Taryn's phone. "I need to get in there."

"After you." Pete held the door for her and motioned Taryn through.

Quinn hadn't exaggerated. The drugstore was wall-to-wall Eagles Nesters of all ages creating cheerful chaos. The jukebox played peppy Christmas tunes and people jiggled in place, but there would be no dancing on the black and white tiled floor today. Most everyone had a soda fountain treat in a to-go cup which they sipped or spooned up while they waited in a line that wound through the store's aisles.

Those who merely wanted to watch, like Taryn and Pete, had the biggest challenge. Only the top of Santa's ornate chair, perched on a raised platform, was visible above the crowd. Mrs. Claus, aka Ellie Mae Stockton, used a bullhorn to keep the proceedings organized.

Pete glanced down at her. "Want something from the fountain?"

She grinned. "And how do you propose to get it if I do? Fly over there?"

"I've noticed there's a system. I give money and my order to someone next to me and they pass it from person to person until it gets to the counter. Eventually the order will get passed back to me."

"I want to order something just to see how that works. A peppermint milkshake, please."

"I'll get one, too. Simpler that way." He handed money to a person standing next to him and like the old game of telephone, the order traveled through the crowd.

"I'm fascinated. When we used to play telephone, the message always ended up garbled. We may not get peppermint milkshakes."

"I hope we do. Now I want one."

"Can you see Gage and Emma in that line?"

"No, but I know he's there. Gonna text him." He took out his phone and sent the message. "Ah. He's fifth in line for Santa."

"That's great but I don't know how we'll ever see it."

"He just explained it. Anyone who goes up and has relatives in the crowd tells Ellie Mae. She'll clear a space for us. When Josh is done, we move out and let others stand there."

"Awesome. This is a lot more organized than it looks."

"That's Ellie Mae for you. Supposedly she worked on the set of several major film productions. When I see something like this, I tend to believe it."

"Two pineapple shakes, coming over."

Pete glanced at the person. "Not peppermint?"

The guy smiled. "I know that's what you ordered, but looks like this is what you got. You okay with that?"

"Yes, we are," Taryn said. "Thank you."

Pete handed her one of the shakes. "Like you said, the telephone game."

"I like pineapple shakes."

"I like 'em, too, but they're not very Christmasy."

"They are if we say they are." She lifted her to-go cup. "*Mele Kalikimaka*."

He laughed and raised his. "*Mele Kalikimaka* to you, too. Ever been to Hawaii?"

"Yes. You?"

"Not yet. And I sincerely doubt I'd go at Christmas, so my knowledge of how to say Merry Christmas in Hawaiian is wasted."

"No, it isn't. We just used it."

"So we did." He smiled and took another sip.

"I keep meaning to ask if you're in the talent show."

"I am."

"Doing what?"

His eyes twinkled. "You'll find out."

"Aww! You're not going to tell me?"

"What fun is that? It's Christmas, the season of surprises. This is just another one." He paused. "Speaking of that, are you in it?"

"Not this year. I'm considering it for next year. Could be extra fun for the Christmas guests if their hostess performs. I plan to get tickets for everyone who registers."

"Good idea. So what's your talent?"

"I have many."

"I know that. I meant what are you—"

"You'll find out."

He laughed. "Nicely played."

"*All relatives of Josh Sawyer, front and center, ho, ho, ho.*"

"That's our cue."

"Except I'm not a relative."

"Doesn't matter. You're with me. And the category's flexible, anyway." Grabbing her hand, he threaded them through the crowd to the front.

"*Move it on back, folks! Josh has a large entourage.*"

"Isn't that the truth." Taryn looked around at all the familiar faces, Sawyers and McGavins mixed together. Badger was there, along with the Bennett family, which was closely tied to the McGavins.

She made sure to give a smile to Uncle Brendan, who returned it before continuing his conversation with Jo Fielding. Josh's loosely defined family included about thirty people.

"He's about to go up." Pete sounded excited. "Would you hold my shake so I can take pictures?"

"Absolutely." Judging from all the phones in the crowd, she'd have no trouble getting copies if she wanted them.

Josh couldn't ask for a more authentic Santa. From the pure white trim on his red velvet suit to the polish on his black boots, he was spectacular. His snowy beard curled just enough and his wire-rimmed glasses perched on his nose at the exact angle to make him look jolly yet wise.

Gage held one of Josh's hands and Emma held the other as Josh toddled up to Santa wearing a green elf costume, complete with hat. He stared up at the man sitting on a large golden chair trimmed with faux jewels.

The crowd went still, as if it was holding a collective breath waiting for the little boy's reaction.

Santa leaned down and held out both white-gloved hands. "Want to come up, Josh?"

Gage and Emma exchanged a glance and let go of his hands, giving him the choice to stay or leave.

"Da-da!" Josh lifted both arms and Santa scooped him onto his lap.

A sigh went up from the crowd and shutters clicked or whirred, depending on how many shots were being taken. Taryn swallowed a giggle. That kiss selfie had forever changed how she viewed the camera on her phone.

Josh patted Santa's face and started to tug on his beard. Santa expertly untangled the tiny fingers. Reaching a mittened hand toward Mrs. Claus, he took the plush reindeer she placed there and gave it to Josh. The little boy hugged his new toy to his chest and made a whinnying sound.

Santa surveyed the crowd and zeroed in on Quinn and Kendra. "In case you didn't get that, he wants a pony."

"We're on it," Quinn said. "Thanks, Santa."

Gage plucked Josh from Santa's lap and the show was over.

"God, he's cute."

Taryn glanced up and her heart squeezed. He sure did love that little kid. Joy shone in his smile and the light in his eyes. She was entranced by both. That was unsettling.

He'd mentioned getting his own house. Did he also want his own family? That wish might not have surfaced, yet, but any man who gazed at a child that way clearly was meant to be a father.

The Pete she'd hired in June had simply been looking for a job. Now, whether he recognized it or not, he was looking for a life.

27

What a great day it was turning out to be. After a quick trip home to feed the horses and drop his duffle inside the front door, Pete handed Taryn back into his truck for the drive to the Guzzling Grizzly. He hadn't been around for last year's Christmas talent show, but he'd seen the videos and had been looking forward to it ever since.

Gage had come up with the Sawyer family act. He'd found an acapella version of *Sleigh Ride* that wasn't too challenging and they'd talked their dad into singing bass.

It wasn't quite Pentatonix, but it didn't suck, either. The five of them used to fool around singing harmony when everyone was still at home. With some practice and a little coaching from Bryce McGavin, they had their chops back.

He'd held off mentioning it to Taryn. At first he hadn't said anything because he wasn't sure it would come together. When it did, he hadn't told her because...yeah, he wanted to impress her. That had likely been his motivation all along.

On the way in, she tried to guess what the act would be. "I doubt you're juggling since Badger's doing that with Ryker and Cody."

"We're not juggling, but there's been a change in their lineup. Luke Bennett's standing in for Cody on the juggling team. Cody's staying home with Faith and Noel."

"Oh, goodness, I forgot about that little baby. Of course they can't bring her into a packed venue when she's only five days old. But it's sad they'll miss it."

"They won't miss it entirely. Everyone will be using their phones to do live video chats with them. It won't be the same, but at least they'll get the gist of the show."

"Well, good. That makes me feel better." She glanced over at him. "Are you doing a dance routine? I've been hearing about the Sawyer dancing tradition."

"We're not tap dancers, if you're picturing top hats and tails."

"So you're wearing what you have on?"

"Yes, ma'am. This act doesn't require a costume. We leave that to the Whine and Cheese Club."

"Do you know what they're doing?"

"I don't, but I think my dad does. He wouldn't tell me. Said it was a state secret."

"For a town where news travels like lightning, keeping these acts under wraps must be a challenge."

"But good marketing. More people buy tickets because they can't stand not being there to see what everyone comes up with. That means more money for needy families."

"I can see that. Besides, I'll bet people want to video Warren Bennett in his Godman spandex and cape, no matter what he does."

"Yeah." Pete chuckled. "Should be great, too. Luke said his dad's been working on his comedy routine since last Christmas."

"Is there a printed program?"

"Nope. That would give too much away. Bryce has a cheat sheet, and that's been closely guarded, too."

"Can you at least tell me how many acts before yours?"

"Two."

"You're the third act? That's terrific."

"And necessary. Gage and Emma are bringing Josh, but they can't stay for the whole thing. After our act, they'll drive to Faith and Cody's and watch with them."

"I guess babies complicate things."

"But they're so worth it."

"Sounds like you're a fan."

"I didn't know I was until Josh showed up. Watching that little guy has been a kick. I'll bet he'll go nuts when he sees his daddy up there performing."

"He won't be the only one going nuts. I can't wait."

"You won't have to much longer. We're here."

The next hour went fast. Dinner was part of the deal so everyone was served from an abbreviated menu. The Sawyers, the McGavins and the Bennetts claimed three large round tables. Each table was a mix of families.

His dad was often the life of the party, but tonight his uncle shared that role. He'd also dived into the great-uncle persona. When Josh grew restless during dinner, Uncle Brendan carried him around the room, introducing him to people and asking how they were enjoying their evening.

Pete had ended up sitting between Taryn and Jo Fielding. At one point, Jo leaned toward him. "Is your uncle always like this?"

"By *like this*, you mean…"

"He acts like he's never met a stranger. He assumes everyone he encounters will love him."

"Then the answer is yes. He's been like that ever since I can remember. He's a card-carrying member of Extroverts Anonymous."

"Except I'll bet extroverts like him are never anonymous."

"That's a fact. They make sure you know their name."

On his other side, Taryn gave him a nudge. "Bryce is coming up to the microphone."

"Then we must be ready to start the show." That gave him a few butterflies, but once he got up there he'd be fine. He wasn't as outgoing as his uncle, but he could handle something like this.

"Love Bryce's outfit."

"That looks like a new one." Bryce was in all white, even his boots. Then Nicole came out in the same dazzling white. "Did you hear their album hit number four on the charts?"

"No, but I'm not surprised. They're quickly converting me into a country fan."

He sent her a quick grin. "I knew there was hope for you." Then he settled back as Bryce welcomed everyone and Nicole announced how much money had been raised. After that they launched into a rendition of *Winter Wonderland.*

They were playing to their hometown crowd and the audience clearly loved every note they sang and every chord they strummed. When they finished, Pete rose to his feet with everybody else. Those two were destined for stardom, but clearly they'd never forget their roots.

Badger, Ryker and Luke stepped up next and executed a dazzling juggling display of holiday plates to Mannheim Steamroller's *Joy to the World.* Pete glanced at Josh, who bounced and clapped all the way through it. Bryce might have put that number second so Josh would be there for it.

Then it was time for the Sawyer contribution. Pete stood, and on impulse leaned down and gave Taryn a quick kiss for luck. His mouth tingled as he joined his brothers, his sister and his dad on stage.

His dad gave them a note on the pitch pipe and they were off on a spirited sleigh ride. Pete tuned into his dad's bass, Roxanne's soprano and Wes's tenor. He and Gage sang baritone, rounding out the quintet.

It worked. For the whip crack, his dad unfurled an honest-to-god whip and cracked it on stage. Like he was Indiana Jones. The ending called for a horse whinny and Gage chimed in with the most compelling whinny a human could possibly make. He'd always been good at it.

Judging from this afternoon at Pills and Pop, he'd been teaching his son. When the cheers and wild applause had died away, Josh was still practicing his whinny. After hugs and high-fives all around, Gage, Josh and Emma left.

Pete settled in his chair next to Taryn and ordered a beer. Adrenaline coursed through his system. They'd done well.

"I absolutely loved that."

He scooted around to face her. "I'm glad. I wanted you to."

"Well, I did. I had no idea you could sing. Or that any of you could."

"We used to for the fun of it. This time we put in some serious practice. Bryce tutored us."

"I hope you keep it up. The five of you were so into it. Fun to watch."

"It was fun to do. Feels like old times."

"I'm happy for you."

"Amazin' job, mate." His uncle arrived and clapped him on the shoulder. "Great to see. Sawyers always have been good singers."

"Do you sing, Uncle Brendan?"

"You don't remember the karaoke machine I brought one Christmas?"

"You were the one who gave us that? I loved that thing."

"Well, I'm the bloke who gave it to the family." Then he turned to Jo. "Ever tried karaoke, lovely lady?"

"A few times."

"Ah, so modest. I'm bettin' you're a wild woman when you get up on that stage."

She smiled. "No, Brendan, I am not. But I'll bet you're a wild man when you get up…on that stage."

"Yea, yea, I have my moments. Anyway, I need to go back to my seat. The next act is about to start. Nice chattin' with you." He tipped his hat and left.

Pete smiled. Uncle Brendan was flirting with Jo and she was flirting right back. Cute. Too bad it wouldn't come to anything since they lived on separate continents.

Now that the Sawyer number was over, Pete could do a little flirting of his own. He and Taryn had turned their chairs around to face the stage. He was close enough to casually drape his arm over the back of hers and lightly caress her shoulder.

She'd worn a white sweater tonight with a snowflake pattern woven into it. Soft. Touchable. She looked great.

Glancing over, she gave him a warm smile.

Happiness poured through him, a river of contentment on the surface with an undercurrent of anticipation for the moment they'd be alone. It would be the icing on the cake of one of the best days of his life.

<u>28</u>

No wonder the talent show had become a favorite event even though this was only its second year. Taryn had missed the community-wide events earlier in the year and she wouldn't miss them again.

Eagles Nest was special. She'd sensed it the first time she'd visited. She'd banked on it when she'd decided to launch her business here. But she hadn't fully experienced the camaraderie that knit the community together until tonight. She'd had a taste of it at the caroling event for Noel McGavin, but the talent show was a banquet of good cheer that she'd never forget.

So much goodwill. So much good-natured laughter. Ellie Mae Stockton came out with a tiny tree she placed on a stool and proceeded to bust some moves as she danced around it to *Rockin' Around the Christmas Tree.* Fire Chief Javier Ortega led his firefighters in a rousing rendition of *Let It Snow! Let It Snow! Let It Snow!*

Then Reverend Warren Bennett strutted on stage in his spandex Godman outfit. The guy could have made it as a standup comic. She laughed until the tears came. When she looked over at Pete, he was in the same condition, out of breath, eyes watering.

The grand finale turned out to be the Whine and Cheese Club's creation. They'd all left their seats some time ago, so Jo's place next to Pete was empty.

His uncle claimed it. "I hear these women are something else."

Pete chuckled. "You don't know the half of it."

"Jo's one of them, right?"

Taryn hid a smile. Uncle Brendan had a crush.

Bryce stepped up to announce that the Whine and Cheese Club would be loosely interpreting *The Twelve Days of Christmas*. "And because the club is only five strong," Bryce said, "they've added seven recruits. You may not recognize some of them under their costumes, but the club wishes to thank Mandy, April, Olivia, Hayley, Ingrid, Abigail and Roxanne, who not only agreed to participate, but helped make the outfits."

Taryn leaned toward Pete. "What a project! And you heard nothing?"

"Nothing." He swiveled in his seat to glance at his dad, who was sitting behind them. "Way to keep a secret, Dad."

"She would have killed me if I'd let anything slip." He made a shooing motion with his hand. "Turn around. You don't want to miss any of it."

The tune started and a woman dressed as a partridge came out juggling pears. Real pears.

Taryn figured that out when she dropped one and one of the servers rushed to clean up the smashed pear. Next came a cooing woman in a turtle dove costume holding a large placard labeled *2*.

Because Quinn was chuckling as the woman cooed, Taryn guessed that the turtle dove was Kendra. The size and shape was right.

The song circled back, allowing the partridge to juggle and drop another pear. The French hen wore a French maid's costume and carried a duster that she used on everyone seated close to the stage. Whoever was under the black calling bird costume held aloft the number *4* while she talked wildly on her cell phone.

Deidre, dressed in a shiny gold jumpsuit, held up the number *5* while twirling a gold hula hoop. Then the audience got involved, belting out *five golden rings* with every repeat.

A tall goose pranced out next with her number *6* held high. When she took her position, she wiggled her butt and pantomimed laying an egg.

Brendan laughed and nudged Pete. "That's Jo," he said in a low voice. "I can tell."

A white swan was the last of the bird costumes, which meant Taryn had a shot at recognizing the rest. Ingrid was the maid-a-milking. She brought out a stool and a pail and set to work.

With each round, the audience shouted *five golden rings* louder than the time before. Abigail presented ladies dancing in a sexy belly dancing routine that drew more whistles. Roxanne was an enthusiastic lord-a-leaping. During one leap, she almost took out Ingrid on her stool.

Badger's sweetheart Hayley loudly played a kazoo for pipers piping. Ryker cheered for April when she walked out wearing a big *12* on her head and rocking the bongos hanging from a strap around her neck. By then the crowd was on its feet as everyone joined in for the big finish.

Taryn cheered until she was hoarse. The twelve women linked hands and took bow after deep bow. At last, blowing kisses, they exited the stage.

"Wow. Just wow." Taryn glanced up at Pete. "So much fun."

"Makes you glad you live in Eagles Nest, doesn't it?"

"Sure does. You couldn't pry me out of here with a crowbar."

He held her gaze, his eyes alight with happiness. "You don't know how glad I am to hear that."

* * *

Rattled by Pete's remark, Taryn had hidden behind small talk as they'd left the GG and got into the frigid cab of his truck. He'd offered to have her wait inside while he warmed up the interior, but she'd scoffed at the idea that she needed coddling.

"It'll warm up soon." He backed out of the parking space. "That's the problem with going out for the evening in winter, especially right after a blizzard."

"When you said it would be cold in the truck I didn't have a clue *how* cold. On the other hand, it's not right for you to brave the frozen interior of your cab while I toast my tootsies in the cozy GG."

"Sure it is. Gives me a chance to show off how tough I am."

"I want to be tough, too."

"You want to show off for me?"

"You bet. I am woman. Hear me roar." Good. They were teasing each other again. Maybe she'd overreacted to his soulful gaze and heartfelt comment a while ago. She reached out and adjusted the vent. "Ah, warm air." She settled back in her seat. "I'm in awe of the pioneers. They had to build a fire if they wanted to get warm."

"Fires are nice, too."

"Why, yes, they are." Time to get their sexy on. "Ours is ready, by the way."

He smiled. "Good to know. Oh, and by the way, while you light the fire, I have a few things to bring in."

"Like what?"

"Nothing much. Tonight's a special occasion, so I thought we should…I don't know…commemorate it."

Or maybe she hadn't overreacted to that moment in the GG. She glanced around the two-person cab. "Where are they?"

"In the truck bed."

Evidently he'd brought surprises and they were too big to shove behind the seat. But maybe they were practical surprises and he was joking about the commemorative part of it. "I know what you got. You found some fancy pulley apparatus for the rope line."

"What we already have should work. I was planning on installing that line tomorrow morning after breakfast."

Or not joking. "Just so you know…" She paused for emphasis. "I have the makings for French toast."

"Do you, now?"

"I thought after we feed and turn out the horses in the morning, we could make the French toast, eat in front of the fire and get…cozy."

"I see." He cleared the huskiness out of his throat. "I guess my rope line project might get moved to later in the day, then."

"Works for me. I can't speak for you, but I don't have anything on my agenda that can't be postponed."

His breath caught. "Sounds like you're looking forward to…everything."

"I am. I was going to surprise you, too, but maybe anticipation is better. I've made up our bed in front of the fireplace."

He gave her a quick glance. "You have?"

"It's ready and waiting for us."

"Alrighty, then." The husky tone was back. "Better get your keys out. Don't want to waste time getting the door open."

"Got 'em." This was more like it. Pulse racing, breathing shallow, looking forward to more of Pete's loving. "I'm ready."

"So am I, lady. So am I."

29

Lord-a-mercy. Pete had been sexually ramped up many times in his life, but never like this. He drove the bumpy ranch road slightly faster than he should have.

He hadn't planned when and how he'd give her what he'd brought, but afterward was fine, especially since she'd made up the bed. When a hot woman was eager for a man's attentions, only a fool would suggest opening presents first. He'd just get everything inside as quickly as he could.

Taryn unlatched her seatbelt before he'd fully stopped, and by the time he switched off the motor she was out the door. He lost gentlemanly behavior points right there, but he likely gained studly behavior points for inspiring her to act that way.

He was also damned inspired as he hopped out of the truck. The Christmas lights in the yard illuminated the tarp, which had a layer of frost on it. Pulling it aside, he lifted out the cooler and set it on the frozen ground.

He stacked the box of gifts on top of the cooler and carried both inside, nudging the door closed with his hip. Then he set everything down and unbuttoned his coat.

Flames licked at the wood arranged in the fireplace. She'd also turned the Christmas tree lights on. Illuminated by firelight and the multicolored glow from the tree, Taryn was undressing.

He shuddered in the grip of fierce desire as she pulled the white sweater over her head and tossed it on the couch. Her coat and scarf lay over the back of it. Her boots were on the floor nearby.

He was out of his coat in record time. Hooking it and his hat on the coat rack, he leaned down and unzipped his duffle. After locating the condoms, he pocketed one.

Then he followed her lead, grabbed the back of the couch and pulled off his boots and socks. His shirt was next, then his t-shirt. He left on his jeans. He needed what was in his front pocket. Didn't want to lose track of it.

By the time he rounded the couch, she'd stripped down to her bra and panties. Black, familiar. The ones he'd plucked out of the washing machine two nights ago. He swallowed. "Did you wear those for me?"

She smiled. "Would I do that?"

"I think you would." He stepped onto the blanket bed she'd arranged. "And then you'd leave them on so I could take them off."

"You're a good guesser." Her hot gaze traveled over him and she sucked in a breath. "That's a nice look on you."

"You, too."

She pivoted gracefully, turning her back to him. "The hooks are tricky."

"I'll see what I can do." She was beautiful from all angles. Tracing a path from the base of her spine to the narrow band of elastic across her back, he flicked the catch open. Then he stepped closer and slid both hands under the loosened cups to cradle her breasts. Her nipples were taut, eager.

He squeezed them gently between his thumb and forefinger as he leaned down to kiss her shoulder. She trembled beneath his touch. "Hooks are undone." He pressed his mouth against her warm skin and licked the curve of her shoulder. "Got any more jobs for me?"

Her voice quivered. "My panties feel a little tight. Would you take them off, please?"

"Sure thing." He brushed the straps of her bra off her shoulders and the sexy lace garment fell to the blanket. Kneeling behind her, he grasped the panties that hugged her hips and drew them slowly down. He kissed the smooth curve of her bottom as he uncovered it, paying equal attention to each cheek.

His aching cock protested, but he was willing to suffer for this. When the flimsy piece of black material dropped to her ankles, she kicked it away.

He circled her waist with both hands. "Turn toward me."

She rotated in his loose grasp, her breath coming faster, her scent driving him crazy. Moving lower and tilting his head back, he coaxed her nearer. There, right there.

He explored with his tongue and she gasped. Went deeper and she moaned. Splaying his fingers over her firm ass, he brought her closer and settled in.

With a soft groan, she abandoned herself to his loving. Tunneling her fingers through his hair, she gripped his head and arched into his caress. Moments later he took her over the edge and her cries of pleasure mingled with the crackle of the fire. Sweet music.

As she quivered in the aftermath of her climax, he guided her down to the blanket. Standing slowly, wincing at the sharp pinch of denim, he unfastened his jeans with a sigh of relief.

His cock sprang free as he shoved off both jeans and briefs. At last. He retrieved the condom, ripped it open and clenched his jaw as he sheathed himself.

Then he glanced at Taryn. Firelight danced over her flushed skin, capturing the sheen of moisture on her breasts and between her thighs.

Her heavy-lidded gaze slid over his aroused body. She drew in a shaky breath and ran her tongue over her lips. "I want you."

Heat settled low in his belly. "I want you, too." He barely recognized the rasping, desperate voice as his. Lowering himself to the blanket, he eased between her thighs. Braced above her, shaking from the force of his need, he covered her mouth with his.

Moaning, she opened to him, clutching his head and welcoming the thrust of his tongue. His heart pounded in anticipation as he gently probed her wet, hot center with the tip of his cock. He entered her slowly, deliberately. His needy body strained at the leash, but he refused to take her like some rutting beast.

Lifting his head, he held her gaze as he pushed deeper. Taking a quick breath, he buried his cock to the hilt. His heart raced and intense pleasure blurred his vision.

Then it cleared and he focused on her beautiful eyes. Every fiber of his being rejoiced in the union of his body with hers, but this was so much more. If he was granted the privilege, he would make love to her many times. But there was only one first time.

Gently he began to move, his gaze locked with hers. Stroking her hands down his back, she clutched his hips, urging him on as her body warmed beneath his. Her eyes grew luminous as she tightened around his cock.

Adrenaline shot through him. Pumping faster, he bore down and she rose to meet his thrusts, pressed her fingertips into his flexing muscles.

Her eyes widened. "*Pete.*"

"I'm here." He gulped for air. "I'm here, Taryn." He drove home once, twice, and she arched upward with a wild cry.

Glorious. As her climax rolled over his cock, he surrendered to his, welcoming the rush, the heat, the pulsing rhythm that blended with hers. So good.

So good that he was at a loss for words. Which was okay because he didn't have enough breath to say anything. Even when he'd dragged in more air and could manage a comment, he failed to come up with a way to express himself. All he could do was smile.

That seemed to be her setting, too. Combing a lock of hair back from his forehead, she sighed in contentment.

"Couldn't have said it better." He brushed a kiss over her smiling lips. "I need to deal with the condom."

"Okay." She propped herself on her elbows. "I'll stoke up the fire."

"Good idea."

"Do you want anything? A beer, maybe?"

"Actually, after I take care of this I'll get out what I brought in from the truck." He started down the hall.

"Refreshments?"

"That's part of it." He ducked into the bathroom. This was working out fine.

When he returned to the living room, Taryn had wrapped in one of the blankets and was curled up on the couch. Even with a fire going, it was too chilly to sit around naked.

"I guess for this part, I'll get at least semi-dressed."

She smiled. "Don't do it on my account."

"Thanks for that. I'm tough, but my family jewels, not so much. They get cold." He quickly pulled on his briefs, jeans and t-shirt. Good enough. He'd be taking everything off again soon, anyway.

Walking over by the door where he'd left the stuff, he set the box of gifts aside and crouched next to the cooler.

"I'm dying of curiosity."

He glanced over. She'd turned and was watching him over the back of the couch. "Like I said, just some little surprises to commemorate tonight." He hoped the champagne was okay after riding in the truck. He and his brothers used to fool around shaking up bottles of it, but usually it settled down again in a few minutes.

He flipped open the cooler lid and everything looked fine. "Guess we'll start with this." Taking out the bottle, he turned toward her. "I figured you had champagne glasses."

"Oh!" She looked startled.

"You don't?"

"No, no, I do. I just wasn't expecting...wow. Champagne. Thank you." She didn't sound delighted, though.

"Do you like it?"

"I do. I love champagne."

"Good. I brought Christmas cookies, too, just wreaths and trees, not Santa or Frosty."

"That's...that's wonderful."

Was it really? Didn't sound like it. "You don't have to eat them now."

"Now's fine. You went to a lot of trouble."

Damn. Not the reaction he'd hoped for at all. "But if you don't want—"

"Let's have the champagne and cookies. I'll bring out glasses and plates." She started to get up.

"I'll do that. Just tell me which cupboard the glasses are in."

She settled back onto the couch. "The one over the stove. You might need to rinse them out. I haven't used them since I moved here."

"I'll do that, then." Bottom line, she wasn't thrilled about the treats and he didn't know why. Otto had thought this was a terrific idea. Maybe she wasn't hungry or thirsty. Maybe just the poinsettia and the gifts would have been a better way to go.

"I have one more thing in the cooler." Setting the champagne bottle on the floor, he took out the poinsettia and adjusted the white and gold bow tied around the pot. Then he stood and carried it over to the couch. "This was so pretty, and I thought it would look nice on..." He froze. "Are you crying?"

"Y-yes." She wiped her face with a corner of the blanket.

"Happy tears?"

She shook her head.

Setting the poinsettia on an end table, he walked around the couch and scooched in beside her. "What's the matter?"

"You're being romantic."

"And that makes you cry?"

She nodded and wiped her eyes again.

"What's wrong with being romantic?"

Tears rolled down her cheeks. "Everything!"

<u>30</u>

"I know you don't get it." A lump of misery sat in Taryn's stomach as she gazed at Pete.

"No, I sure don't. You'll have to explain it to me."

"We're risking a lot as it is. If you go adding this kind of thing—" She gestured vaguely to the poinsettia.

"It's just a holiday plant. No big deal."

"It is a big deal! So is the champagne, the cookies and whatever's in that box." She dragged in a breath. "You're changing the game."

Emotion flickered in his eyes. "It's not a game. At least not to—"

"I used the wrong word. It's not a game to me, either. But it can turn into a trap. The first few months with Rafael were filled with romantic gestures—moonlight and champagne, lovely flowers, soft guitars."

"So let's trash the poinsettia and break out the beer. If I'd known those things would stir up bad memories, I never would have—"

"That's just it. I love poinsettias. I love champagne. I just don't want them to *mean* anything."

His voice was soft. "Why not?"

Good question. She scrambled for a coherent answer. "It just... complicates things. It's the wrong trajectory. If we can stick with just the physical attraction, then—"

"Hold it." His jaw clenched. "All you want from me is sex?"

"No!" She stared at him in dismay. "We have so much more than that! We work well together, we understand each other—"

"Could've fooled me."

Ouch. "Maybe not about this, but about the ranch, the horses, the fun of creating something that others will enjoy." She sent him a pleading glance. "I think of you as a friend."

Gradually the tight muscles in his jaw relaxed and his gaze mellowed. "Same here. Which I happen to think is our greatest asset. I see it as a foundation for building...something more."

Exactly. She swallowed. "And I see the potential for it blowing up in our faces."

"Really?" He studied her. "After seven months of daily interaction? That's what you imagine will happen?"

The discussion seemed doomed, but she'd give it one more shot. "We've been getting along well because we've kept things light and breezy. I was hoping we could continue doing that."

His gaze searched hers. "Light and breezy."

"Yes."

"No substance to it."

"You make it sound like all I want is a surface relationship."

"Because that's what I'm hearing. But I don't believe a word of it. Not after making love to you on that blanket two nights ago and again tonight." Tension roughened his voice. "We passed light and breezy a long time ago, but we absolutely left it behind the night of the blizzard. If you're not allowing yourself to see that, then—"

"All I see is danger!" Her heart hammered. "I'm doing my best to warn you, but you're not listening! You—"

"Tell you what." He stood. "I'm going home. Let the dust settle. I'll be back in the morning to feed."

"That's too soon. We need more time."

He took a deep breath. "Then you call it. You're the boss."

"Pete! Please don't—"

"Just an expression. But the truth is, you are in charge of how this goes. I've played my cards. You know where I stand."

Her brain wasn't firing on all circuits, but he was right. The next move was hers. "It's the holidays. You should take extra time off."

"That's BS."

"Okay, then, I need time alone."

He inclined his head. "Now we're getting somewhere."

"Then I'll see you at Wild Creek Ranch on Christmas Eve."

"We were planning to come back here at midnight and go down to the barn."

"I know."

"Of course, you don't need me there. You can visit the barn without me."

"I don't think so." She was confused about a lot of things, but not that. "We should go together. See if the horses have anything to say."

"All right." He walked toward the door. "I'll pick up the cooler later."

"Okay."

He eyed the box as he put on his coat and hat. "As for the rest, you can open it, toss it in the trash, give it to charity. Whatever you want. It's yours." He walked out the door, closing it quietly behind him. Moments later, his truck started. Gradually the rumble of the engine grew fainter. He was gone.

Well, she'd certainly mucked that up. But better to screw up an evening than let him continue down the road to disaster. Was she a ratfink for spoiling his celebration plans? Maybe. Was it the right move? Only time would tell.

She stared at the box he'd left behind. Nothing good would come from opening it. But it wasn't in her nature to throw away a gift unopened. He'd made the effort to get her something. She could at least look at it.

A shipping label on the box was addressed to his dad. Pete had likely repurposed the box to haul over whatever he'd bought her. It wasn't heavy but the cardboard was chilled from being outside. She had to clutch it against her body to keep her blanket from sliding to the floor as she carried it over to the couch.

Popping open the interlocked flaps, she looked inside and counted four packages wrapped in John Deere paper. If he'd gone with a tractor theme, opening the gifts would be even tougher.

She pulled away the tape on a small, floppy package and took out a dark green John Deere knit hat. Her heart gave a painful twist. Yep, this was gonna be hell. Might as well dive into the boiling cauldron and get it over with. When she tugged on the hat, the stretchy material molded to her head like a caress.

The next package was an instructional DVD on tractor driving. He'd put a sticky note on it—*Because I don't know everything.* She wiped her eyes on the blanket. She'd get through this. Then she could cry.

To hell with being careful with the paper, though. She ripped open the third one and discovered a pair of John Deere customized driving gloves. They fit perfectly.

She left them on as she opened the biggest, heaviest gift, which was in a box with a cellophane window. Her chest hurt so bad. Undoing the flap, she pulled out a detailed metal replica of a John Deere tractor and held it in her lap. Okay, now she was gonna cry.

* * *

What was that awful noise? Head pounding, she sat up. Her phone alarm. Cripes, what a disgusting tune. She poked the screen so hard the phone went spinning to the floor.

Oh, great. Probably cracked the screen. And the stupid alarm was still going. Flipping on the light, she squinted in the glare. She was changing that alarm chime ASAP.

Climbing out of bed was a chore. Either her head was too heavy or her neck was too weak. Either way, she was compelled to hold onto her head to keep it steady. Any sudden movement drove icepicks into her brain. Evidently eating sugar cookies and chugging an entire bottle of champagne before going to bed had been a very bad move.

Leaning over to get the phone would be torture. Might as well leave it there. She managed to pull on her bathrobe and shove her feet mostly into her slippers. Then she left her bedroom and closed the door so she wouldn't hear the chime.

Coffee. Aspirin. Shower. *Get it together, kid. The horses need to be fed and you're the only one around to do it.*

About three hours later, she was recovered enough to eat a little breakfast, drink more coffee and take stock. She hadn't cracked the screen on her phone, thank goodness.

Interacting with the horses had been a bittersweet experience. The activity was so tied in with Pete. Those critters probably wondered what was up with all the hugging, but wrapping her arms around their sturdy necks and laying her cheek against their silky coats centered her.

Mucking out stalls ended up being good therapy for her hangover. Who knew? She'd tackled the job with a vengeance and worked up a sweat that prompted her to drink lots of water.

She'd washed and put away the blankets. Then she'd cleaned out the fireplace and laid kindling and logs on the andirons because that was her habit. Might not be easy to sit in front of the fire by herself tonight, but she'd do it.

Loading the dishwasher with her breakfast dishes took care of her immediate chores. Too bad, because she desperately needed something to do. Maybe she should put up a few more holiday decorations.

She wasn't in the mood, but she had more ribbons and other odds and ends stored in a box. She hadn't used her collection of pinecones, either. Extra greenery was available right out the front door. She'd put on holiday music. She'd be merry and bright, doggone it!

The process worked like a charm. She loved so much about this time of year—the carols, the festive decorations, the beloved traditions. She'd be adding a new one this year by going to the barn at midnight on Christmas Eve. Since Pete had told her about it, sharing the moment with him was the right thing to do.

Eventually she ran out of spots that needed a festive bow or a cluster of pinecones and greenery. She was especially proud of the centerpiece she'd created for the dining table using the poinsettia, greenery, pinecones, and tapers of red, green and white.

Time to put any leftover items away and feed the horses. She'd never found a use for the skeins of yarn, one red and one dark green, that she'd bought a couple of years ago. Hadn't found a use this year, either.

Or had she? Before she headed down to the barn, she tucked the yarn and a pair of scissors in a canvas bag and took it along. Then she added a small cellophane bag of baby carrots. She'd never braided a horse's mane and tail, but how hard could it be? Her efforts didn't have to last through a parade, only through Christmas Eve.

After bringing the horses in from the pasture and delivering hay flakes all around, she pulled out her phone, accessed the Christmas music she had stored there and chose one of her favorite albums, *Celtic Christmas.* The flutes, violins and soft vocals created a serene atmosphere as she cut lengths of red and green yarn and tucked them in one jacket pocket. Carrots went in the other.

When Honey Butter, the first one fed, had finished his dinner, she walked into his stall and gave him a couple of carrots. "Tomorrow night is Christmas Eve, buddy. I'd like to spruce you up for that special event. Are you with me?"

The palomino eyed her for a moment before nuzzling her pocket for more carrots.

"I'll give you another one when we finish." She stroked his velvet nose and evaluated his cream-colored mane. "You can help by standing still." Starting at the top of his neck, she finger-combed a section, divided it into three strands and began.

Whether it was the music or the sensation of fooling with his mane that calmed him, the gelding stood quietly as she worked. She finished her first braid and tied a bow of red yard at the end to hold it.

Stepping back, she smiled in satisfaction. "Not bad. Pete is going to be so surprised when he sees this."

Honey Butter snorted and bobbed his head.

"Speaking of that cowboy, my plan to keep things casual fell apart last night."

Shifting his weight, the palomino let out a gusty sigh.

"Yep, not good." She tied green yarn to her second braid. "He wants deep and meaningful. In my experience, that gets you into trouble." She finished a third braid and tied it with red yarn.

"All that romantic stuff is distracting. Like I completely ignored how different Rafael and I were. He procrastinated on everything. I'm an ASAP person. Our body clocks were incompatible. Lark versus owl. Ditto with our sense of humor. I could go on, but you get the idea, right?"

The gelding snorted.

"Exactly." She braided another section. "Pete thinks it's time to get serious. I don't agree. It's too risky. And way too soon. We could end up regretting it like Rafael and I did because we rushed into something we weren't ready for."

Pete's words came back to her. *After seven months of daily interaction? That's what you imagine will happen?*

"You tell me, Honey Butter. Wouldn't you say there's a huge difference between working with someone for seven months and dating them for seven months? Our first kiss was only five days ago, for heaven's sake."

No response. She tied on another bow and peered at the horse's heavy-lidded eyes. "Are you falling asleep on me?"

He slowly turned his head in her direction and his expression was so blissed out it made her laugh. "Clearly this routine works for you."

His head was drooping by the time she finished the last braid. "You look very handsome and very sleepy, my friend. Here's your reward, a bedtime snack." She gave him one more carrot. The lazy crunch of his teeth made her giggle as she left his stall.

Each of the other horses reacted much the same way Honey Butter had. The combination of music and having their manes braided lulled them into a semi-trance. She left the barn smiling.

Pete was going to love those Christmas-themed manes. Too bad he hadn't been there to witness how mellow those critters had become during the process. He would have gotten such a kick out of—

She came to an abrupt halt between the barn and the house. She was right about how Pete would react to this impulsive project of hers. She was right because they'd spent seven months together—working, arguing, planning, laughing, and last of all...making love.

We passed light and breezy a long time ago, but we absolutely left it behind the night of the blizzard.

Clearly he had. But what about her? She hadn't left anything behind. She was stuck in the past, clinging to old fears. He'd invited her to step into a very special future. Did she have the courage to accept?

31

The Wild Creek Ranch house was roomy, but it bulged at the seams on Christmas Eve. Pete sipped a beer and talked with Ryker and April about their chickens, which had been in residence for a year. Those two were enamored of their laying hens, so conversation flowed easily.

Pete was grateful for that. The evening had been somewhat of a chore to get through. He and Taryn had exchanged a polite greeting and he'd worked at avoiding her after that.

Should have been easier than it was considering all the folks packed into the house. Inevitably, though, he ended up brushing past her to help himself to food or heard her laughter not three feet away.

He'd always looked forward to Christmas Eve, and up until Saturday night, he'd been super excited about it this year. Having his entire family in one place, including Uncle Brendan, promised to be a blast and a half. Adding in the McGavin crowd had expanded his anticipation to epic proportions. Then...Taryn. Intense joy had disintegrated into anxiety.

He didn't do anxiety well. He preferred action. And he couldn't take any, at least not where Taryn was concerned. On Sunday, he'd given his dad and uncle a quick summary, followed by a request to drop the subject when he was around.

The family grapevine had clearly been busy since then because no one asked an awkward question or made a painful reference. He supposed they'd all had practice at this. In a blended family of this size, issues were bound to crop up. His with Taryn was just the most current one.

He did his best to concentrate on the good stuff going on in this room. Cody and Faith had brought Noel and after a brief show-and-tell moment, they'd tucked her in a back bedroom.

She was a cute little thing. So tiny. She'd inherited her mom's blond hair. Her eyes would be light, but no telling if they'd end up green like Faith's or McGavin blue.

Josh had held court earlier, too, but now that it was past eleven, he was fast asleep in the crib Kendra had provided. Emma ran a tight ship with that little kid. Bedtime was firm, even on Christmas Eve.

Mandy, Zane's wife, had provided the biggest news. She and Zane were expecting a baby in July. Jo hadn't been able to stop talking about it all night. Fun to see how excited she was about being a grandma.

Kendra had recently joined the conversation about chickens and was discussing egg size when Pete's dad tapped on his beer bottle with a spoon to get everyone's attention.

"I've maintained a Christmas Eve tradition in my family for years, and Kendra's agreed to go along with it."

Bryce spoke up. "Is this the thing about talking horses?"

"Yep. Folk legend says that at midnight the horses in the barn are given the gift of speech. Crazy as it sounds, Kendra and I will bundle up in about fifteen minutes and walk down to the barn, the older one, and listen."

"I'm going, too," Jo said. "I believe."

Uncle Brendan raised his beer. "Yea, yea, I'll be there."

"Great. Anyone else who wants to come along is welcome. You can sing carols on the way if you want, but keep your voices down once you get in the barn, please."

Pete looked for Taryn. She glanced over at him and raised her eyebrows, asking a silent question. He gave a quick nod. He hadn't told his dad about this development. He'd been prepared for Taryn to change her mind. Better alert him now.

After working his way through the crowd, he tapped his dad on the shoulder. "Forgot to mention something. I told Taryn about the horses talking and she wants to listen to hers. I said I'd go with her. Evidently she still wants me there."

His dad's gaze was thoughtful. "That sounds like a good idea."

"I have no idea if it will be or not."

"Hey, what's this? Where's my positive thinker?"

Pete had no answer for him.

"Christmas Eve is a magical time, son." He gave Pete's shoulder a squeeze. "Keep your heart open."

Pete had been maintaining his cool, but that comment got to him. Swallowing the sudden lump in his throat, he nodded and went to find Taryn.

She was talking with Emma, but she excused herself and walked to meet him. "We should go."

"I just told Dad."

"Let me thank Kendra for tonight and I'll meet you by the front door. I left my purse in the truck. My coat's somewhere on that rack."

"The white one or the parka?"

"The parka. I knew I'd need that when we go to the barn."

"I'll have it ready for you." His heart was racing by the end of that short, totally informational conversation. God, he wanted to do this for her without making a damn fool of himself.

He located his jacket and hat first, and then unearthed her coat. It was a wonder the wooden coat tree hadn't tipped over under the weight.

He'd put his jacket on and was ready to help her into hers when she showed up, pink-cheeked and breathing faster than normal. As he held the coat, she slid her arms into the sleeves and thanked him.

"You're welcome." He waited for her to zip up before he opened the door. "Better put on your gloves, too."

"Right." She tugged them out of her pocket. "Let's go."

He opened the door and followed her out. His body registered the cold and he could see his breath, but he was too wired to care about the temperature. "Where are you parked?"

"To the right, over by the barbeque area."

"Lead the way."

"Oh, you don't have to—"

"Lead the way." Some things were non-negotiable.

She shoved her gloved hands in her pockets and headed toward the barbeque area. "I love the John Deere stuff."

Wham. Right in the heart. "That's good."

"The hat and gloves fit great."

"I'm glad." He stepped around her so he could open her door and help her in. Her hand in his nearly undid him. "Pull out and wait for me. I'll be right behind you." He closed her door quickly, before he said something stupid.

Jogging to his truck helped. Movement of any kind was welcome. He backed out, wheeled around and drove up behind her. She blinked her lights and started down the Wild Creek Road.

The drive over to her place took forever, although the clock on his dash recorded less than fifteen minutes. She drove straight to the barn and he parked right beside her.

She was out before he could get to her, which wasn't surprising. "I'll bet the horses will wonder what the heck is going on."

They're not the only ones. She could have cancelled this program at any time. Why hadn't she? Her original decision to stick with the plan could have been a knee-jerk reaction, but upon further reflection, she could have begged off.

But no, here they were, standing in front of her barn at five minutes to midnight. He slid the bar across and opened the door, letting her go first. Then he stepped in and closed it behind them. The aisle lights gave the barn a soft, warm glow but not enough to see anything clearly.

"I'm thinking we should leave it like this." She walked over to Honey Butter's stall. "If we turn on the overheads, they might not talk."

Despite the tension wrapped around his chest like a steel band, he smiled. "They might not talk anyway."

"I know. The thing is, I wanted you to see what I did, but I'm not sure if you can in this light."

"What did you do?"

"Come over and look at Honey Butter. Maybe when your eyes adjust, you'll be able to see."

He approached the stall. "What am I looking for?"

"Last night I braided his mane and tied the braids with red and green yarn."

"That's awesome." He concentrated on the palomino. "I can tell his mane's braided. Can't see the colors, though."

"Belatedly I realized that you wouldn't be able to without the overhead. I did the same thing with all of them."

"Really?" He took that as a positive sign even though he couldn't have said exactly why.

"You can check it out in the morning."

"You want me here in the morning?"

"Yes, please."

Another positive sign. Could be super positive but he wouldn't get ahead of himself. "Then I'll be here."

She lowered her voice. "I think he's asleep."

"I doubt it."

"He's so quiet."

"He might be dozing, but I guarantee they're all aware that we're here."

"I guess they would be. They can hear like nobody's business." She turned in his direction. "Where do you want to be?"

Now there was a question. *In your arms.* "I'll just stand by you, if that's okay."

"I'd like that."

He decided not to ask why. It was almost midnight. If they were going to do this right, they had to be quiet.

"How long should we listen?"

"That's up to you."

"How long do you usually wait to see if they'll say anything?"

"I'm good for about five minutes. I figure if they are given the gift of speech, they'll either use it right away or decide it's not worth the effort."

"Then five minutes it is." She pulled her phone out of her pocket. "Almost time." She cleared her throat. "It's midnight."

He kept his breathing as quiet as he could and not because he wanted to hear the horses speak. For the first time since he'd been doing this, he didn't care what the horses did or didn't do. He focused on Taryn's breathing.

It wasn't smooth and regular. It had a little catch to it, as if she might be agitated. The scent of her perfume mingled with the familiar aroma of hay and horses. She didn't normally wear perfume when they were in the barn together.

But she'd dressed for a party, with makeup and another nice sweater, this one green. John Deere green, to be more specific. Interesting that she'd liked what he'd bought. What if he'd skipped the champagne and flowers and only given her the John Deere stuff? Would that have made a difference?

Damn, five minutes was a long time, especially when he was within touching distance. Okay, when five minutes were up, he'd ask her why they were here. Or why *he* was here. That was the critical—

"Time's up. I didn't hear any horses talk. Did you?"

"No, ma'am." He paused. "I just have to ask. Why am I here?"

She turned to face him. "Because I wanted to be the first person to wish you Merry Christmas."

"Uh, okay. Merry Christmas to you, too."

She took a step closer. "And because Christmas is a great time to get clear on things."

"Is it?" His heart beat a rapid tattoo.

"For me, anyway. When I was braiding Honey Butter's mane, I told him all the reasons why I didn't want to get serious about you."

"And?" He could barely breathe. *Please don't let me be dreaming this.*

"To borrow your words, it was all BS."

"Oh?"

"I'm serious about you. I have been for a long time. I love you, Pete."

He sucked in air. "Taryn..." He started toward her.

She held up her hand. "Wait a sec. Once you kiss me, it's all over. I need to say this. I've been falling for you ever since we met. But like an idiot, I wouldn't—"

"I know. I get it. Doesn't matter."

"It does matter. I acted like all the time together didn't count. I was so wrong. Every day, every hour, every minute I spent with you led to our first kiss."

"Do you think maybe it could lead to another one? Because I'm going crazy over here."

"Sure. I think that's the gist of what I needed to say."

"Thank God." He eliminated the distance between them and swept her into his arms. "I love you so much." He lowered his head. "So very much." He settled down lightly, still not quite believing that he was awake.

But she didn't disappear. Instead she wrapped her arms around his neck and kissed him back with so much enthusiasm that he groaned and pulled her in tighter.

A much louder groan sounded nearby. Then a nicker came from another stall. One of the horses blew air through his nostrils and another stomped his hoof.

He discovered it wasn't easy to kiss a laughing woman, so he gave up, because it was pretty damn funny and he loved hearing her laugh.

"Pete, the horses are talking."

"Yeah, they are."

"I even know what they're saying."

"Oh?"

"They're saying *hey, you two, get a room.*"

He grinned. "Think we could find one on Christmas Eve?"

"I think so. It so happens I know the innkeeper."

"Lucky me, so do I." And he dived in for one more hot kiss before hustling her out of the barn and across the frozen ground to her house, lit up with dozens of sparkling white lights. On his way, he glanced up at the night sky filled with stars, including one that was especially bright. Just like his dad had predicted, magic was happening.

Epilogue

Didn't get any better than this. Brendan had enjoyed some amazing Christmas celebrations, but spending the big day at Wild Creek Ranch topped them all. The huge family Quinn had latched onto was worth the price of admission. Brendan had been impressed with the food and good cheer at the Christmas Eve bash, but Christmas dinner was even better.

Or maybe it seemed that way because he'd learned everyone's name and had all the connections straight. Or maybe it had to do with his nephew Pete, who looked happier than a koala with a handful of gumtree leaves.

Whatever had happened at midnight in Taryn's barn had done that boy a world of good. Could be whatever had happened after midnight, too, judging by his besotted expression. Made Brendan a little wistful, although he wouldn't trade places with the kid. Forty-nine suited him fine and he wasn't afraid of the big five-oh, either. Maturity had its advantages.

For example, a younger man might not appreciate the lovely attributes of Jo Fielding. She was tall, lithe and sexy as hell. Whenever he flirted with her, she gave as good as she got. And yet...beneath her bravado and quick wit lurked a touch of uncertainty.

Quinn had filled him in on a few details about her divorce some thirteen years ago. But Quinn was protective of Jo and clearly wouldn't stand for anyone messing with her. She was Kendra's best friend. Jo's daughter Mandy, the latest mother-to-be, was married to Kendra's son Zane. Anyone interested in Jo would do well to keep those parameters in mind.

Brendan was interested. More than he cared to admit. Her uninhibited laughter drew his attention from across the room. He'd caught himself staring like a stunned mullet at the graceful curve of her neck and the movement of her fingers as she stroked the stem of her wineglass while she talked.

Quinn, his ever-vigilant older brother, had cornered him later in the day over by the Christmas tree. "Everything okay?"

"Couldn't be better."

"Just thought I'd ask. You've been exceptionally quiet today. Couldn't help wondering why." His gaze was direct.

Brendan gave him a big smile and clapped him on the shoulder. "Just soakin' up the holiday ambiance, big brother. Takin' it all in."

* * * * *

Confirmed bachelor Brendan Sawyer has been two-stepping away from Cupid's arrow for years. But a visit to the cozy town of Eagles Nest and an introduction to the lovely Jo Fielding has snared his wandering boots, turning him into the perfect target in A COWBOY'S CHOICE, book thirteen in the McGavin Brothers series!

* * * * *

New York Times bestselling author Vicki Lewis Thompson's love affair with cowboys started with the Lone Ranger, continued through Maverick, and took a turn south of the border with Zorro. She views cowboys as the Western version of knights in shining armor, rugged men who value honor, honesty and hard work. Fortunately for her, she lives in the Arizona desert, where broad-shouldered, lean-hipped cowboys abound. Blessed with such an abundance of inspiration, she only hopes that she can do them justice.

For more information about this prolific author, visit her website and sign up for her newsletter. She loves connecting with readers.

VickiLewisThompson.com

Lightning Source UK Ltd.
Milton Keynes UK
UKHW040908190620
365202UK00001B/163